No man should be that gorgeous.

She tore her gaze away from his smile. Unfortunately, she was immediately snagged by his glossy black hair, thick-lashed brown eyes, tanned skin with a faint beard shadow despite the early hour, handsome features....

Were all the Fortune men this blessed by nature? she wondered. If so, God help the women who caught their attention—because females didn't stand a chance against all that powerful, charming, handsome male virility.

Perhaps she was fortunate that he was her boss and thus off-limits. Never mind the fact that he was also not interested in her.

Because if he ever turned that undeniable charm on her, she'd give in without a whimper.

Dear Reader,

I love children of all ages but I'm especially fond of toddlers. So when I was asked to be part of this FORTUNES OF TEXAS series with a story that included one-year-old triplets, my response was "YES!" How much fun would this be? It turned out to be even more than I had anticipated—especially when those three darling babies were paired with Nick, a handsome bachelor who's clueless about children. Fortunately for both Nick and the triplets, a baby-friendly heroine comes to their rescue. And like famous nanny Mary Poppins, Charlene brings warmth, love and organization to their lives.

I hope you enjoy reading this story as much as I enjoyed writing it—and for any mother reading this who actually has triplets in their family, please take a bow and accept my heartfelt amazement. You're Supermom!

Warmly,

Lois Faye Dyer

TRIPLE TROUBLE

LOIS FAYE DYER

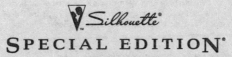

Silhouette®

SPECIAL EDITION®

Published by Silhouette Books

America's Publisher of Contemporary Romance

Special thanks and acknowledgment
to Lois Faye Dyer for her contribution to the
Fortunes of Texas: Return to Red Rock miniseries.

 **SILHOUETTE BOOKS**

Recycling programs
for this product may
not exist in your area.

ISBN-13: 978-0-373-65439-0
ISBN-10:   0-373-65439-1

TRIPLE TROUBLE

Visit Silhouette Books at www.eHarlequin.com

Printed in U.S.A.

Books by Lois Faye Dyer

Silhouette Special Edition

Lonesome Cowboy #1038
He's Got His Daddy's Eyes #1129
The Cowboy Takes a Wife #1198
The Only Cowboy for Caitlin #1253
Cattleman's Courtship #1306
Cattleman's Bride-to-Be #1457
Practice Makes Pregnant #1569
Cattleman's Heart #1611
†*The Prince's Bride* #1640
*Luke's Proposal #1745
*Jesse's Child #1776
*Chase's Promise #1791
*Trey's Secret #1823
**The Princess and the Cowboy #1865
†*Triple Trouble* #1957

*The McClouds of Montana
**The Hunt for Cinderella
†Fortunes of Texas: Return to Red Rock

LOIS FAYE DYER

lives in a small town on the shore of beautiful Puget Sound in the Pacific Northwest with her two eccentric and loveable cats, Chloe and Evie. She loves to hear from readers and you can write to her c/o Paperbacks Plus, 1618 Bay Street, Port Orchard, WA 98366. Visit her on the Web at www.LoisDyer.com and www.SpecialAuthors.com.

For Grant Suh and his proud parents, Steve and Brenda.
Welcome to America and our family, Grant—
we're so glad you're here.

Chapter One

Nicholas Fortune closed the financial data file on his computer and stretched. Yawning, he pushed his chair away from his desk and stood. His office was on the top floor of the building housing the Fortune Foundation, and outside the big corner windows, the Texas night was moonless, the sky a black dome spangled with the faint glitter of stars.

"Hell of a lot different from L.A.," he mused aloud, his gaze tracing the moving lights of an airplane far above. The view from the window in his last office in a downtown Los Angeles high rise too often had been blurred with smog that usually blotted out the stars. No, Red Rock, Texas, was more than just a few thousand miles from California—it was a whole world away.

All in all, he thought as he gazed into the darkness, he was glad he'd moved here a month ago. He'd grown tired of his job as a financial analyst for the Kline Corporation in L.A. and needed new challenges—working for the family foundation allowed him time to contemplate his next career move. And a nice side benefit was that he got to spend more time with his brother, Darr.

With the exception of the hum of a janitor's vacuum in the hallway outside, the building around him was as silent as the street below. Nicholas turned away from the window and returned to his desk to slide his laptop into its leather carrying case. He was just shrugging into his jacket when his cell phone rang.

He glanced at his watch. The fluorescent dials read eleven-fifteen. He didn't recognize the number and ordinarily would have let the call go to voice mail, but for some reason he thumbed the On button. "Hello?"

"Mr. Fortune? Nicholas Fortune?"

He didn't recognize the male voice. "Yes."

"Ah, excellent." Relief echoed in the man's voice. "I'm sorry to call so late, but I've been trying to locate you for three days and my assistant just found this number. My name is Andrew Sanchez. I'm an attorney for the estate of Stan Kennedy."

Nicholas froze, his fingers tightening on the slim black cell phone. "The *estate* of Stan Kennedy? Did something happen to Stan?"

"I'm sorry to be the bearer of unfortunate news." The caller's voice held regret. "Mr. Kennedy and his wife were killed in a car accident three days ago."

Shock kept Nicholas mute.

"Mr. Fortune?"

"Yeah." Nicholas managed to force words past the thick emotion clogging his throat. "Yeah, I'm here."

"It's my understanding you and Mr. Kennedy were quite close?"

"We were college roommates. I haven't seen Stan in a year or so, but we keep in touch—*kept* in touch by phone and e-mail." *Like brothers,* Nicholas thought. "We were close as brothers in college."

"I see. Well, Mr. Fortune, that probably explains why he named you guardian of his children. The little girls are currently safe and in the care of a foster mother, but the caseworker is anxious to transfer custody to you. The sooner they're in a stable environment the better."

"Whoa, wait a minute." Nicholas shook his head to clear it, convinced he hadn't heard the attorney correctly. "Stan left *me* in charge of his kids?"

"Yes, that's correct." The attorney paused. "You didn't know?"

Nicholas tried to remember exactly what Stan had told him about his will. They'd both agreed to take care of business for the other if anything happened to them. He'd been Stan's best man at his wedding to Amy and he definitely remembered Stan asking him to look after his bride should anything happen. Even though their conversation had taken place while emptying a magnum of champagne, Nicholas knew his word was important to Stan and he hadn't given it lightly.

But *babies?* And not just one—*three.*

"The triplets weren't born when we made a pact to look after each other's estate, should anything ever happen," he told the attorney. *And neither of us thought he and Amy wouldn't live to raise their daughters.* "But I promised Stan I'd take care of his family if he couldn't."

"Excellent." The attorney's voice was full of relief. "Can I expect you at my office tomorrow, then?"

"Tomorrow?" Nick repeated, his voice rough with shock.

"I know it's extremely short notice," Sanchez said apologetically. "But as I said, the caseworker is very concerned that the babies be settled in a permanent situation as soon as possible."

"Uh, yeah, I suppose that makes sense," Nick said. He thrust his fingers through his hair and tried to focus on the calendar that lay open on his desktop. "I've got a meeting I can't cancel in the morning, but I'll catch the first flight out after lunch." Nicholas jotted down the address in Amarillo and hung up. It was several moments before he realized he was sitting on the edge of his desk, staring at the silent phone, still open in his hand.

Grief washed over him, erasing the cold, numbing shock that had struck with the news. He couldn't believe Stan and Amy were gone. The couple met life with a zest few of their friends could match. It was impossible to get his head around the fact that all their vibrant energy had been snuffed out.

He scrubbed his hand down his face and his fingers came away damp.

He sucked in a deep breath and stood. He didn't have time to mourn Stan and Amy. Their deaths had left their three little girls vulnerable, without the protection of parents. Though how the hell Stan and Amy had ever decided he was the best choice to act as substitute dad for the triplets, Nicholas couldn't begin to guess.

In all his thirty-seven years, he'd never spent any length of time around a baby. He had four brothers but no wife, no fiancée or sister, and his mom had died two years ago. The only permanent female in his immediate family was Barbara, the woman his brother Darr had fallen in love with a month earlier. Barbara was pregnant. Did that mean she knew about babies?

Nick hadn't a clue. And for a guy who spent his life dealing with the predictability of numbers, in his career as a financial analyst, being clueless didn't sit well.

But he had no choice.

Despite being totally unqualified for the job, he was flying to Amarillo tomorrow.

And bringing home three babies.

He didn't know a damn thing about kids. Especially not little girls.

He was going to have to learn fast….

Charlene London walked quickly along the Red Rock Airport concourse, nearly running as she hurried to the gate. The flight to Amarillo was already boarding and only a few stragglers like herself waited to be checked through.

Fortunately, the uniformed airline attendant was efficient, and a moment later, Charlene joined the short queue of passengers waiting to board.

For the first time in the last hour, she drew a deep breath and relaxed. The last three weeks had been hectic and difficult. Breaking up with her fiancé after three years had been hard, but quitting her job, packing her apartment and putting everything in storage had been draining. She'd purposely pared her luggage down to a few bags, since she'd be living with her mother in a condo in Amarillo while she looked for a job and an apartment.

And a new life, she told herself. She was determined to put her failed relationship with Barry behind her and get on with her career.

She sipped her latte, mentally updating her résumé while the line moved slowly forward. They entered the plane and her eyes widened at the packed cabin and aisle, still thronged with passengers finding seats and stowing bags in the overhead compartments.

Thank goodness I used my frequent flyer miles to upgrade to first class. She glanced at her ticket and scanned the numbers above the seats, pausing as she found hers.

"Excuse me."

The man rose and stepped into the aisle to let her move past him to reach the window seat.

He smelled wonderful. Charlene didn't recognize

the scent, but it was subtle and clean. Probably incredibly expensive. *And thank goodness he isn't wearing the same cologne as Barry,* she thought with a rush of relief.

She was trying to get away from Barry—and didn't need or want any reminder of her ex-boyfriend. Or fiancé. Or whatever the appropriate term was for the man you'd dated for three whole years, thinking he was the man you'd marry, until you'd discovered that he was…not the man you'd thought he was at all.

Very disheartening.

"Can I put that up for you?"

The deep male voice rumbled, yanking Charlene from her reverie.

"What?" She realized he was holding out his hand, the expression on his very handsome face expectant. He lifted a brow, glanced significantly at her carry-on, then at her. "Oh, yes. Thank you."

He swung the bag up with ease while she slipped into the window seat. She focused on latching her seat belt, stowing her purse under the seat and settling in. It wasn't until the plane backed away from the gate to taxi toward the runaway that she really looked at the man beside her.

He was staring at the inflight magazine but Charlene had the distinct impression he wasn't reading. In profile, his face was all angles with high cheekbones, chiseled lips and a strong jawline. His dark brown hair was short, just shy of a buzz cut, and from her side view, his eyelashes were amazingly long and thick. She wondered idly what color his eyes were.

She didn't wonder long. He glanced up, his gaze meeting hers.

Brown. His eyes were brown. *The kind of eyes a woman could lose herself in,* she thought hazily.

His eyes darkened, lashes half lowering as he studied her.

Charlene's breath caught at the male interest he didn't bother to hide. Her skin heated, her nipples peaking beneath the soft lace of her bra.

Stunned at the depth of her reaction, she couldn't pull her gaze from his.

Despite his preoccupation with what lay ahead of him in Amarillo, Nicholas couldn't ignore the quick surge of interest when he looked up and saw the woman standing in the aisle.

When he stood to let her reach her seat, she brushed by him and the scent of subtle perfume teased his senses. The sleek fall of auburn hair spilled forward as she sat, leaning forward to slide her purse beneath her seat. She tucked the long strands back behind her ear while she settled in and latched her seat belt.

Finally, she glanced sideways at him and he was able to catch a glimpse. Her thick-lashed eyes were green as new spring grass. They widened as she stared at him.

She wasn't just pretty. She was beautiful, he realized. And if the faint flush on her cheeks was any indication, she was feeling the same slam of sexual awareness that had hit him like a fist the moment her gaze had met his.

"Everything okay?" he asked when she continued to stare at him without speaking.

She blinked, and just that quickly the faintly unfocused expression was gone, replaced by a sharp awareness.

"Yes." She lifted one slender-fingered hand in a dismissive gesture. "I had to nearly run to catch the plane. I hate being late."

Nicholas nodded and would have said more, but just then the plane engines throttled up, the sound increasingly louder as the jet hurtled down the runaway and left the tarmac. He glanced at the woman beside him and found her gripping the armrests, eyes closed.

Clearly, she didn't like to fly. Air travel didn't bother Nicholas, but he waited until the plane leveled out and her white-knuckled grip relaxed before he spoke.

"I'm Nicholas." He purposely didn't tell her his last name. The Fortune surname was well-known in Red Rock and being part of a rich, powerful family carried its own problems. He'd learned early that many people associated the name with a preconceived set of expectations.

"Charlene London," she responded as she took a bottle of water from her bag. "Are you flying to Amarillo on business?" she asked, sipping her water.

"Not exactly." He paused, frowning.

Charlene tucked an errant strand of hair behind one ear with an absentminded gesture. *What did that mean?* "I see," she said.

He laughed—a short, wry chuckle. "I don't mean to be vague. My trip is both business and personal."

"Oh." Curious though she was, Charlene was reluctant to grill him. Somewhere in the coach section of the airplane, a baby began to cry.

Nick stiffened and appeared to listen intently until the cries turned to whimpers. Tension eased from his body and he looked at her, his gaze turbulent.

"My college roommate and his wife died a few days ago and I'm guardian of their daughters. I'm going to Amarillo to take custody of three kids. Triplets." He sighed. "Twelve-month-old triplets."

Charlene's eyes widened with shock. She was speechless for a moment. "You're kidding," she finally managed to get out.

"Nope." His expression was part gloom, part stark dread. "I'm not kidding."

"Do you and your wife have children of your own?"

"I'm not married. And I don't have any kids," he added. "The closest I've ever come to having a dependant is my dog, Rufus."

"So you'll be caring for three babies...all by yourself?"

He nodded. "That's about the size of it."

"That's crazy."

"Yeah," he said with conviction. "Insane."

"I'm the oldest of six siblings, two of whom are twins," Charlene said. "If you'd permit a little advice from someone who's been there—you should hire a full-time nanny, and the sooner the better."

Nicholas thought she probably was right—in fact,

the more he considered the idea, the more he was convinced. Before he could ask her more questions, however, the woman walking the crying baby up and down the aisle reached their row.

"Excuse me." Charlene stood.

Nicholas wanted to ask her if she knew anything about hiring nannies, but her abrupt request stopped him. He stepped into the aisle to let her pass him. Her shoulder brushed his chest in the slightest of touches, yet his muscles tensed as if she'd trailed her fingertips over his bare skin.

Nick dragged in a steadying breath, but it only served to flood his senses with the scent of subtle perfume and warm woman.

He nearly groaned aloud. He'd dated a lot of women over the years, but he hadn't reacted to a female with the level of gut-deep, instant lust since he was a teenager. He blinked, frowned and ordered his rebellious body to calm down. He couldn't afford to be distracted just now—he had to focus on dealing with Stan and Amy's little girls.

He dropped back into his seat. He expected Charlene to walk toward the lavatories at the front of the first class section, but instead, she waited until the young mother turned and moved back down the aisle.

"Hi," Charlene smiled at the weary mother. "I bet you're exhausted."

Oh hell. Nick tensed when the woman holding the baby looked like she was going to cry. He hated it when women cried. Fortunately, the woman didn't burst into tears.

"I'm beyond exhausted," the woman murmured, patting the wailing baby on the back soothingly. "And so is she," she added. "I don't think either one of us has slept more than a half hour at a time for days."

"Oh my. My little brother did the same thing," Charlene said, her gaze warm and sympathetic. "He was born several weeks premature and had acid reflux. Poor little guy. It took a while for us to figure out how to handle him so he could fall asleep."

The young mother's eyes widened. "You found a solution? What was it?"

"I'd be glad to show you," Charlene said, holding out her arms.

The woman hesitated, clearly torn about handing her baby to a complete stranger.

"I totally understand if you're not comfortable with having me hold her, after all, we don't know each other," Charlene said reassuringly. "I could try to explain, but it's much easier to demonstrate."

The baby chose that moment to wail even louder than before. The unhappy cry seemed to galvanize the mother, because she eased the tiny little girl off her shoulder and passed her carefully to Charlene.

Nick didn't know much about babies, but every one he'd seen had been cradled or propped against someone's shoulder. Charlene did neither. Instead, she laid the baby facedown on her arm, the little head in the palm of her hand, and gently swayed her back and forth while smoothing her free palm over the tiny back. The baby's arms waved jerkily, slow-

ing in time with her cries that quickly gave way to hic-
cupping sobs, then blessed silence.

Nick stared at Charlene. *Damn. She's good.
Really good.*

He glanced at the baby's mother and found her expression as surprised as he felt.

"How in the world did you do that?" she whispered.

"Experience," Charlene murmured, her fingertips
continuing to gently rub in soothing circles over the
little girl's back. The pink cotton dress matched the
baby's sock-covered feet, now dangling limply on
either side of Charlene's arm. "I was twelve when
my little brother was born." She glanced down at the
baby, fast asleep and seemingly boneless in her arms.
"If you tilt her slightly to the right when you hold her,
change her diaper or feed her, it helps with acid
reflux too. I don't know if your little girl has that
problem, but if she does, the pain can make her so
uncomfortable that she won't be able to fall asleep
or stay asleep."

"Thank you so much." The words carried a wealth
of heartfelt appreciation as she carefully took the
sleeping baby from Charlene.

"You're welcome," Charlene replied, moving
aside to let the mother and child step past her. She
watched them move down the aisle and return to
their seat in coach.

Nick stood to let Charlene slip into her seat near
the window, then dropped into his own.

"Impressive," he told her. "Very impressive."

She shrugged and picked up her water bottle to sip. "Basic stuff, if you've ever helped care for a baby. Unfortunately, most new moms only find out about the little things to make life easier for them and their baby if they talk to someone who's coped hands-on with the problem."

After watching Charlene's easy confidence with the crying baby before she handed the peacefully sleeping child back to her mother, Nicholas knew he'd found the answer to his urgent need for a nanny. "Makes sense. Experience always counts. I need someone with that level of experience. How about you?" he asked.

"How about me…what?"

"Being the nanny for the triplets. I'll pay you double whatever the going rate is," he went on when she shook her head.

"I'm sorry, I really am. But I'll be looking for a job in Amarillo."

"What if I offered you a substantial signing bonus—say, twenty-five thousand dollars?"

Her eyes widened. "That's a very generous offer—and one that guarantees applicants will be standing in line for the position. You'll have your pick of nannies. You don't need me."

"Yes, I do." Nick was convinced. Charlene didn't appear to share his opinion, however. "In fact, I'm so sure you're the only person for the triplets that I'll add another twenty-five thousand dollar bonus if you stay until their aunt is found and comes to get them."

She stared at him for a loaded moment. "Their aunt is taking them?"

Nick was surprised she didn't ask about the money, but if she wanted information about the babies, he'd give it to her. "I don't have permanent custody of the girls, only temporary care until the estate locates Amy's sister, Lana. She's a teacher, and according to Amy, a career volunteer with various organizations overseas, helping children in third world countries. She's also married." Unlike me, he thought. A confirmed bachelor with no plans to marry anytime soon. "So the girls will have two parents instead of only me."

"I see."

For a brief moment, Nick thought Charlene was going to accept his offer. But then she shook her head.

"I'm sorry, especially since I know how difficult it is to care for more than one baby. But I have plans and I've made promises to people. I can't let them down on such short notice."

"You're sure I can't change your mind?"

"No, I'm afraid not."

"Too bad." He pulled a business card and pen from his inner jacket pocket and wrote on the back of the card. "This is my cell phone number, in case you reconsider the offer. I'll be in Amarillo until tomorrow, when I have reservations to fly the girls back to Red Rock."

"You aren't staying in Amarillo very long," she commented as she took the card, tucking it into her purse without reading it.

"No. I want to take the triplets home as soon as possible and get them settled in. I doubt anything will make this easier for them, but I thought the faster I transfer them, the better." He pointed at her purse where his card had disappeared. "Call me if you change your mind."

"I'll keep your card," she replied. "But I don't think it's likely I'll change my mind."

They parted in the terminal, Nicholas heading for the exit and Charlene moving to baggage pickup.

Saying goodbye felt wrong. Charlene had to force herself not to turn around and give him her phone number, ask him to call…plead until he promised to meet her later.

Her level of conviction that Nick was somehow important to her was profound.

This is crazy. She held her chin up and kept walking, but her thoughts continued to tumble, one over the other, refusing to leave Nick even as she physically moved farther away from him.

She'd never felt anything approaching the instant attraction that had flared between them, her nerves shaking with need during that first long exchange of glances. Lust and sexual attraction were far more powerful forces than she'd imagined. The time spent sitting next to Nick during the flight had given her new insight into just how intensely her body could respond to the right man. Those moments were forcing her to reevaluate whether she'd ever truly been deeply moved before—including with Barry, she realized with sudden shock.

Yet she'd become engaged to Barry, she reminded herself in an effort to regain control of her emotions.

Clearly her wisdom in this area wasn't infallible. Besides, a man was the last thing she needed or wanted in her life right now. She definitely didn't need the complication of a man who was about to become an instant father to three little girls.

Still, she'd been impressed with Nicholas's willingness to take on the babies. She couldn't help but compare his heroic, stand-up attitude with her ex's lack of responsibility. She couldn't imagine Barry in Nicholas's situation. She seriously doubted Barry would have agreed to take custody of three children. He was adamantly opposed to becoming a parent. It was one of the issues they couldn't agree on, since she very much wanted children—an issue that, ultimately, had caused her to conclude they were completely mismatched.

Charlene collected her three suitcases and stepped out of the crowd of passengers to pull a jacket from inside the smallest bag. March in chilly Amarillo was a far cry from the warmth of Red Rock, located in southern Texas near San Antonio. Sure enough, when she wheeled her bags outside, she was glad she had the added protection of the coat. She tucked her chin into the shelter of her collar and halted to scan the line of cars crowding the curb.

"Charlene! Over here!" Her mother's voice carried clearly over the hum and chatter of passengers.

Charlene returned Angie's enthusiastic wave and hurried down the walkway.

"Mom, it's so good to see you." Charlene basked

in her mother's warm hug, breathing in the familiar scent of Estée Lauder perfume.

"It's been too long," Angie said, scolding with a loving smile as she stepped back, holding Charlene at arm's length. Her eyes narrowed as she swept a swift glance over her daughter, from her toes to the crown of her head. "You're too skinny."

Charlene laughed. "You always say that, Mom. I've lost inches but not pounds—I've been working out at the gym."

"Well, now that you're home, I'm going to feed you," Angie declared firmly.

They loaded Charlene's bags into the trunk. Moments later, Angie expertly negotiated traffic as they left the airport.

"Are you enjoying being in the condo, or do you think you'll miss having a big yard this summer? You spent hours gardening at the old house, and I know you loved the flowers." Charlene's mother had sold the rambler where she and her siblings had grown up after her parents' divorce three years earlier. Following college graduation and Charlene's move to Red Rock, Angie had insisted she should be the one to travel for visits to her six children, especially Charlene, since her job as a Health Unit Coordinator at the hospital E.R. kept her so busy. As a result, Charlene had only seen her mother's condo on two short weekend trips.

"I love condo life," Angie said with a happy smile. "I still garden, but now I'm planting flowers and herbs in terra cotta pots on the lanai. Of course," she added. "I still have to mow the strip of grass in my backyard, but it's tiny compared to the big lawn at the old house."

Angie's voice rang with contentment. Charlene knew what a difficult time her mother had had after the divorce, and was immeasurably relieved that she appeared to have adjusted so well.

"I'm glad you're enjoying it, Mom." She tucked a strand of hair behind her ear and adjusted her Ray-Bans a little higher on her nose to better block the late afternoon sun. "What are you doing with all your free time, now that you're not mowing grass and pulling weeds?"

"I've been busy at work," Angie began before pausing to clear her throat. "And…I've met some-one," she blurted.

Surprised, Charlene looked at her mother and was startled to see a hint of color on her cheeks. "That's great, Mom. Who is he?"

"His name is Lloyd Weber and he's an architect for a firm here in Amarillo. We met playing bridge. I joined the group about six months ago."

"So, you're dating?" Charlene could hardly get her mind around the image of her mother dating. Not that she objected—in fact, she'd urged her mom to get out and about. Angie was fifty-two and loved people and social interaction; Charlene truly believed her mom would be happier in a committed relation-ship.

"Well, yes—we've been dating for a while." Angie pulled up in front of the condo building and parked.

Her expression reflected concern and a certain trepidation when she unlatched her seat belt and half-turned to meet Charlene's gaze. "I didn't tell you before, because…well, because I wasn't sure whether Lloyd and I were going to become serious. But two weeks ago he moved in with me."

Charlene stared at her mother, stunned. "You're living together?"

"Yes, dear."

"Here in your condo?"

Angie nodded. "His house is being remodeled before he puts it on the market, and he was staying in a bed-and-breakfast. I told him it was silly to spend all that money when we're together nearly all the time anyway. I convinced him to move in here."

"Well, um." Charlene managed to say. "That's great, Mom. If he makes you happy, I'm delighted."

"You're not upset?"

"Mom, of course I'm not upset." Charlene hugged Angie. "I think it's great." She sat back, laughing at the sheer relief on her mother's face. "If he's a great guy who's being good to you and you're happy, then I'm thrilled for you."

"I'm very happy, and he *is* a great guy," Angie said firmly. "Now come on, let's get your things inside so you can meet him."

Charlene followed Angie up the sidewalk, towing a rolling suitcase behind her.

What am I going to do now? The question made her feel totally selfish in light of her mother's transparent happiness. But Charlene's practical side told her the situation required a change of plans. She couldn't stay at the condo with her mother and Lloyd during what was surely the honeymoon stage of their relationship.

She needed a new plan. And fast.

What the hell was I thinking?

Nick strode away from Charlene and didn't look back. The airport wasn't crowded and it was a matter of moments before he reached the exit doors and walked outside. He knew it was the worst possible time to meet a woman who interested him. And Charlene London was too pretty to hire as a nanny.

He was going to have enough problems dealing with the sea change about to happen in his life. He didn't need to move a sexy, gorgeous woman into his house to complicate life even more.

He spotted a uniformed driver holding a sign with his name in big block letters, and changed direction to reach the black Lincoln Town Car. During the drive to Andrew Sanchez's office, he scanned a file with information about Stan and Amy's estate the attorney had asked the driver to give him.

Andrew Sanchez was a rotund, balding man in his mid-fifties. Businesslike and efficient, he still exuded an air of concern and sympathy.

"Do you have family or friends available to help with the triplets?" he asked Nick as they concluded their meeting.

"No, but I'm planning to find a nanny. Until then

I have a housekeeper, and she's agreed to work longer hours until I can find someone."

"You might want to consider two nannies," Mr. Sanchez commented. "Those three little girls are dynamos." He grinned with wry affection. "I'm glad you're a younger man, because just spending an hour with them at their foster home wore me out. You're going to need all the energy you can muster."

Nick nodded. He didn't tell the older man that he had no clue how much energy one little girl required from a caretaker, let alone three of them at once. "You're continuing to search for Amy's sister?"

The attorney nodded. "I've hired a detective agency to look for her. They told me they can't give us a time frame, since she's out of the country, but at least Amy's e-mail files gave us the name of the mission organization in Africa that employed her. It's a place to start hunting." He sighed. "The e-mail records on Amy's computer indicate her sister stopped communicating a month or so ago. Also that Amy had been trying to contact her but had no success."

"Any idea why?"

"Lana and her husband apparently resigned their positions with the relief agency where they were employed. But we don't know where they went after that. And given that the two are working in a remote area of Africa, well…" Sanchez spread his hands and shrugged. "It's anyone's guess where they've gone or how long before they surface. As I said, the detective agency warned me they can't guarantee a time frame for locating the couple."

"Let's hope they find her soon. I have to believe Amy's sister and her husband will be better at caring for three little girls than I am."

"The important thing is that you're willing to try." The attorney shook his head. "The interim foster home where the girls are staying is a good situation, but they can't stay there indefinitely. They'll be much better off with you while we're searching for their aunt."

"I hope you're right." Nick wasn't convinced.

It was after 6:00 p.m. before the attorney and Nick finished going over the will and other documents.

"I took the liberty of booking a room for you in a nearby hotel," Sanchez told him as they pushed back chairs and stood. "I understand the triplets are in bed for the night by 7:00 p.m. I thought you might want to wait until morning to see them."

"I appreciate it." Nicholas held out his hand. "Thanks for everything."

"You're welcome." The attorney's clasp was firm. "Let me know if there's anything else I can do for you. And I'll notify you as soon as I receive any information as to the whereabouts of Amy's sister."

Nick walked to the door. "It seems odd to pick up the girls and leave Amarillo without saying goodbye in some way."

"I know." The attorney nodded. "But their wills were very specific. As the closest living relative, Amy's sister will organize a memorial service so friends can pay their respects when she returns."

"I'm damned sure neither of them ever thought

they'd die together and leave the kids," Nick muttered, almost to himself.

"No one ever does." Sanchez shook his head. "It's a hell of a situation. We'll just have to do the best we can and search diligently for the children's aunt."

"Right." Nick said goodbye and left the office to climb into the town car once more.

The conversation with Andrew Sanchez had driven home the unbelievable fact that Stan and Amy were gone. Nick barely noticed the streets the limo drove down as they headed toward the hotel.

Despite his conviction that Charlene wasn't the best choice for an employee on a purely personal level, he definitely believed her experience made her the perfect woman to care for Stan's daughters. Before he unpacked his bag in the hotel room, he called his office in Red Rock and asked his assistant to run a preliminary employment check on Charlene London.

Just in case, he told himself, *she called and said yes to the job offer.* He knew the fact that she hadn't given him her contact number made the likelihood a million-to-one shot—but he was a man who believed in luck.

And he was going to need a boatload of luck to get through the next few days, or weeks, or however long it took before the triplets' aunt showed up to claim them.

Chapter Two

The following morning, the same limo driver picked Nick up promptly at 9:00 a.m.

"We're here, sir." The driver's voice broke Nick's absorption in memories and he realized they were parked in front of a white rambler with a fenced yard and worn grass. It looked lived-in and comfortable.

"So we are," he muttered.

"Mr. Sanchez told me to wait and drive you all to the airport when you're ready, sir."

"Good, thanks," Nick said absently, focused on what awaited him within the house.

A round young woman in jeans and green T-shirt answered his knock, a little girl perched on her hip.

"Hello, you must be Nick Fortune. I'm Christie

Williams. My husband and I are…were friends of Stan and Amy. We volunteered to be temporary foster parents for the girls. Come in."

She held the door wide and Nick stepped over the threshold into a living room, the green carpet strewn with toys. Two babies sat on the floor in the midst of the confusion of blocks, balls, stuffed animals and brightly colored plastic things that Nick couldn't identify. The girls' black hair and bright blue eyes were carbon copies of the child on Christie's hip, who stared at him with solemn interest.

A woman in a gray business suit rose from the sofa as he entered.

"Mr. Fortune, it's a pleasure to see you." She stepped forward and held out her hand, her grip firm in a brief handshake. "I'm Carol Smith, the caseworker. As you can see, the girls are doing well."

Nick nodded, murmuring an absent acknowledgment, his attention on the two little girls seated on the floor. Both of them eyed him with solemn, bigeyed consideration. They were dressed in tiny little tennis shoes and long pants with attached bibs, one in pale purple, one in pink. He glanced at the baby perched on the foster mother's hip. She wore the same little bibbed pants with tennis shoes, only her outfit was bright yellow.

"They're identical?" He hadn't expected them to look so much alike. If it wasn't for the color of their clothes, he wouldn't be able to tell them apart.

"Yes, they are," Ms. Smith replied. "It's quite rare, actually. In today's world, many multiple births are the result of in vitro procedures and the children are more commonly fraternal twins or triplets. But Jackie, Jenny and Jessie are truly identical."

"I see." *Great. How am I going to tell them apart?*

"Fortunately, Amy had their names engraved on custom-made bracelets for each of them. She and Stan didn't need to use them, of course, but any time the triplets had a babysitter, the bracelets were immensely helpful," the foster mother added. "This is Jackie." She shifted the little girl off her hip and handed her to Nick.

Taken off guard, he automatically took the child, holding her awkwardly in midair with his hands at her waist.

Jackie stared at him, blue eyes solemn as she studied him, her legs dangling. She wriggled, little legs scissoring, and Nick cradled her against his chest to keep from dropping her.

She responded by chortling and grabbing a fistful of his blue polo shirt in one hand and smacking him in the chin with her other. Startled, Nick eyed the little girl who seemed to find it hilarious that she'd found his chin. She babbled a series of nonsensical sounds, and then paused to look expectantly at him.

He looked at the foster mother in confusion. "What did she say?"

The woman laughed, her eyes twinkling. "I have no idea. She'll be perfectly happy if you just respond in some way."

"Oh." Nick looked down into the little face, still clearly awaiting a response. "Uh, yeah. That sounds good," he said, trying his best to sound as if he was agreeing with an actual question.

Jackie responded with delight, waving her arms enthusiastically and babbling once again.

Five minutes of this back and forth and Nick started to feel as if he were getting the hang of baby chat.

"Do they know any real words?" he asked the two women after he'd taken turns holding each of the little girls and had exchanged similar conversations with Jenny and Jessie.

"Not that I've heard," Christie volunteered. "But at twelve months, I wouldn't expect them to, necessarily."

Nick nodded, watching the three as they sat on the floor, playing with large, plastic, red-and-blue blocks. Jenny threw one and the square red toy bounced off his knee. He grinned when she laughed, waving her hands before she grabbed another block. She tossed with more enthusiasm than accuracy and it flew across the room. Clearly disappointed, she frowned at him when he chuckled.

"They're going to be a handful," he murmured, more to himself than to the two women.

"Oh, they certainly will be—and are," Christie agreed. "Have you hired a nanny to help you care for them?"

"Not yet. I called a Red Rock employment agency this morning, but they didn't have anyone on their books. They promised to keep searching and call the minute they find someone." Nick glanced at his watch. "I have reservations for a noon flight."

"You're going to fly the girls back to Red Rock?"

Nick switched his gaze from the girls to Christie. Her facial expression reflected the concern in her question.

"I'd planned to." He didn't miss the quick exchange of worried looks between the foster mother and social worker. "Is there a problem with taking the girls on an airplane?"

"I'm just wondering how you're going to juggle all three of them, let alone their luggage, stroller and the carry-on bags with their things." Carol Smith pointed at the corner of the living room closest to the outer door. The area was filled with luggage, a large leather shoulder bag, toys and three ungainly looking children's car seats. A baby stroller for three was parked to one side.

"All of that belongs to the girls?" Nick rapidly considered the logistics, calculating what needed to be moved, stored, checked at the gate before the flight. "I can load their things into the back of the limo and get a redcap at the airport."

"Well, yes, you can," Christie agreed. "But Jessie has an ear infection and is taking antibiotics plus Tylenol for pain, and I'm not at all sure the pediatrician would approve of her flying. And even if he okayed the trip, you'd still have to take care of all three of them on the flight, all by yourself." She eyed him dubiously.

"Is that an insurmountable problem?" he asked.

"For one person, it certainly could be," Carol Smith put in. "Especially when one of them needs a diaper changed or if they all are hungry at once."

"Is that likely to happen?"

"Yes," the two women said in unison.

"I see." Nick really was beginning to see why the women seemed dubious. Maybe they were right to be apprehensive about his ability to care for these kids. Just transporting three babies was going to be much more complicated than he'd anticipated. On the other hand, he'd organized and directed programs for large companies. How hard could it be to handle three little kids?

"You two have a lot more experience at this than me. Do you have any suggestions?"

"If I were you," Christie said firmly, "I'd rent a car and drive back to Red Rock. And I'd hire someone to make the trip with me, because I can't imagine any possible way you can do this without at least one other person to help."

Nick instantly thought of Charlene and wished fervently that he'd gotten her phone number. But he had no way to contact her, *and besides,* he thought, *she'd sounded definite when she'd turned down his offer of employment as the girls' nanny.*

He ran his hand over his hair, rumpling it. "Unless one of you is prepared to volunteer, I'm afraid I'm on my own."

"Is there a family member who could fly here and drive back to Red Rock with you?"

"Maybe." He considered the idea, realizing that he had no other choice. "But it will take time to locate someone, and they probably couldn't get here until tomorrow at the earliest. I'd like to get the girls home and settled in as soon as possible."

The three adults had identical frowns on their faces as they observed the triplets who were happily unaware of the life decisions being considered.

Nick's cell phone rang, breaking the brief silence. He glanced at the unfamiliar number in his Caller ID and nearly ignored it. Instinct, however, had him answering the call.

"Hello." The female voice was familiar. "This is Charlene London."

While eating dinner with her mother and Lloyd, Charlene had felt distinctly like a fifth wheel.

She liked Lloyd and it was clear the man adored Angie. Her mother also clearly felt the same about the charming, gray-haired architect.

Which delighted Charlene. But it left her with a serious problem. Her plan to live with her mother while she searched for a job and an apartment of her own was no longer plausible. But Angie was sure to object if she abruptly changed her plans, and Charlene strongly suspected Lloyd would feel as if his presence had forced her from the condo. *He really is a nice man,* she thought, smiling as she remembered the besotted look on his face when he'd gazed at Angie over dessert.

She knew any one of her sisters or brothers would welcome her into their homes, but they all led crowded, busy lives. She really didn't want to choose that option, either.

What she really needed was an instant job—and a place to live that wouldn't make her mother or Lloyd feel guilty when she left.

"I could take Nicholas's job offer," she murmured to herself. Having retired to her bedroom early, she donned her pajamas. "But that means going back to Red Rock."

She didn't want to return to Red Rock. She wanted a new start, far enough away so there was no possibility she would run into Barry and his friends while shopping, dining out, running errands, or any of the dozens of activities that made up her normal life.

She slipped into bed and spent an hour trying to read, but her concentration was fractured as she continued to mull over her changed situation.

The antique clock in the hallway chimed midnight. Charlene realized she'd spent the last hour lying in the dark, unsuccessfully trying to sleep. She muttered in disgust and sat up to switch on the bedside lamp. It cast a pool of light over the bed as she tossed back the covers and padded barefoot across the carpet to retrieve Nicholas's card from her purse.

The phone number on the back of the card was written in decisive, black slashes. Charlene flipped the square card over to read the front and gasped, feeling her eyes widen.

"Nicholas Fortune?" She stared at the logo on the business card. "He's a member of the Fortune family?" Stunned, she considered the startling information.

Nicholas's status as part of the prominent family eliminated many of her concerns. There was little likelihood she'd run into Barry if she worked as a live-in nanny for one of the Fortunes. The two men moved in far different circles. Which put a whole new slant on the possibility of going back to Red Rock, she realized.

It also explained why he'd offered a two-part employment bonus. Fifty-thousand dollars was probably small change for one of the Fortunes.

She tucked the card carefully into her purse and turned out the light. Working for Nicholas could turn out to be the opportunity she'd been looking for.

On the other hand, how would she deal with her attraction to him? Would she end up sleeping with him if she lived in his house to care for the babies?

She frowned, fingertips massaging the slight ache at her temples.

Surely she could handle living in close quarters with a handsome, sexy man for a few weeks, she told herself. And, given Nick's good looks and probably wealth, he no doubt had beautiful women by the dozens waiting for him to call.

No, it wasn't likely she needed to worry about Nick making a pass at her. The real question was, could she maintain a purely professional attitude toward him?

When she thought about the bonus he'd offered, she could only conclude she needed to set aside any emotional elements and make a purely practical decision.

The following morning, she waited until she'd showered and broke the news to her mother and Lloyd over breakfast before calling Nicholas.

"Hello."

The deep male tones shivered up her spine, and for a brief second she questioned the wisdom of agreeing to work for a man as attractive as Nicholas Fortune. Then she reminded herself just how badly she needed this job. "If it's not too late, I'd like to take you up on your offer of the nanny position," she said briskly.

"You're hired. How soon can you be ready to leave?"

"Almost immediately—I didn't unpack last night. What time is your flight?"

"Change of plans. I'm not flying the triplets back to Red Rock, we're driving."

"Oh."

"Give me your address and I'll pick you up as soon as I have the car loaded."

Charlotte quickly recited her mother's address and said goodbye. For a moment, she stared at her pink cell phone.

Have I just made a colossal mistake?

At the sound of his deep voice, she'd felt shivers of awareness race up her spine and tingle down her arms to her fingertips.

Then she remembered Barry, and her body instantly calmed as if the reaction to Nicholas had never happened. She wasn't ready to be attracted to another man. All she had to do was remind herself of her poor judgment and disappointment with Barry and she was safe, she realized with relief.

Reassured, she set her nearly full suitcase on top

of the bed and tucked her pajamas into it. A quick
trip into the bathroom to collect her toiletries, and she
was ready to face her mother and Lloyd.

Squaring her shoulders and drawing a deep
breath, she slung her purse over her shoulder, picked
up her two bags, and headed downstairs.

Across town, Nick wrestled with the complexities
of fastening three car seats into the SUV the rental
company had delivered. Fortunately, the vehicle was
big enough to have a third seat section and had
enough room for an adult to sit between two of the
triplets, if necessary.

At last, the babies' car seats were securely locked
in place and the bags and boxes filled with the
triplets' clothes, toys and food were packed into the
back of the SUV. The girls were buckled into their
seats, each with a treasured blanket and a favorite
stuffed toy in her arms, and their foster mother tear-
fully kissed them good-bye. Nick had a brand-new
appreciation for the details of traveling with three
babies when he finally pulled away from the curb.

Fortunately for him, the girls all fell asleep within
minutes of driving off.

*The motion of the car must lull them to sleep.
Good to know.*

If they had trouble sleeping at his house, he
realized, he could always drive them around his
neighborhood.

But he knew figuring out this clue about the
babies wasn't enough to make him a reliable substi-

tute parent. If he and the triplets were going to survive until the attorney located Amy's sister, he'd need all the help he could get.

Charlene London was his ace in the hole. He was convinced she had the expertise that he knew damn well he lacked.

He hoped to hell he was right, because he was betting everything on her ability to handle the triplets. If he was wrong, this road trip was going to turn into a nightmare.

Nick's relief at the triplets falling peacefully asleep didn't last long. The girls all woke when he reached the address Charlene had given him and the SUV stopped moving. They immediately began to loudly protest being buckled into their car seats. Charlene said goodbye to her mother and friend in the midst of chaos.

Ten minutes after pulling away from the curb, Nick was no longer convinced he'd found the magic bullet to lull the babies asleep. They cried and fussed nonstop, despite the motion of the SUV.

Several hours of driving south and many miles later, Nicholas turned off the highway into a rest stop and parked. The sun shone brightly, but the afternoon air was still chilly. He left the engine running and the heater on to keep the interior as comfortable as possible for Jenny and Jackie while Charlene changed Jessie's diaper. The little girl lay on the leather seat, kicking her bare legs with obvious delight while Charlene stood in the open V of the door.

Despite the churning little legs, Charlene deftly removed, replaced and snugly fastened a clean disposable nappy.

"I've done my share of tailgating at football games, but this is a new experience," Nick commented as Charlene pulled down Jessie's knit pants and snapped the leg openings closed.

"You're in a whole new world, Nick." She lifted the little girl into her arms, tickling her. Jessie chortled and Charlene laughed. They both looked up to grin at him.

Nick shook his head. Crazy as it seemed, he could swear their faces held identical expressions of feminine wisdom and mystery. "I'm not sure I'm ready for a new world," he murmured as he took the diaper bag from Charlene and returned it to the storage area in the back of the SUV. "I'm getting some coffee," he said, louder this time, so Charlene could hear him. "Want some?"

"Yes, please, I'd love a cup."

Nick crossed the patch of grass between the curb where he'd parked the SUV and the concrete apron surrounding the low-roofed building housing the restrooms. Volunteers manned a small kiosk on one side and offered weary travelers coffee and cookies.

By the time he slid behind the steering wheel again, Charlene had Jessie fastened into her car seat and was buckling her own safety belt. She took the foam cup he held out to her and sipped.

"How bad is it?" he asked, unable to look away from the sight of the pink tip of her tongue as she licked a tiny drop of coffee from the corner of her mouth.

"Not too bad."

He lifted an eyebrow but didn't comment.

"Okay, so it's not Starbucks," she conceded with a chuckle. "But it's coffee and I need the caffeine. I was awake late last night and up early this morning. I really, really need the jolt."

Nick glanced at his watch as they drove away from the rest stop. "The attorney told me the girls are in bed and asleep by seven every night. You're the expert, but I'm guessing it might be a good idea to find a motel earlier rather than later so we can keep them on schedule, if possible."

"I think that's an excellent idea." She glanced over her shoulder at the triplets' drowsy faces. "If we stop earlier, we'll have time to feed them, give them baths, and let them play for a little while before tucking them in for the night."

The motel Nick pulled into was just off the highway. Behind the motel, the tree-lined streets of a small town were laid out in neat blocks, and fairgrounds with an empty grandstand were visible a dozen or so blocks away. Nick was familiar with the motel chain and, as he'd hoped, the staff assured him they could accommodate the needs of three babies.

With quick calculation, he asked for two connecting rooms—one for the girls and Charlene, and one for him. He hoped the babies would sleep through the night.

Not for the first time, he thanked God Charlene had agreed to be the girls' nanny. If he could manage to ignore the fact that she was a beautiful woman, she made the perfect employee.

"If we both carry the girls in first, I can transfer the luggage while you keep an eye on them in the room," he told Charlene when he returned to the SUV. "We're on the ground floor, just inside the lobby and down the hall."

He handed her a key card. "Why don't you carry Jessie, I'll take Jackie and Jenny."

After unhooking the girls and handing Jenny to Nick while he held Jackie, Charlotte lifted Jessie and followed Nick into the motel.

"Our rooms are through there." He led the way toward the hallway on the far side of the lobby.

Distracted by her view of his back, Charlene forgot to reply. Beneath the battered brown leather jacket, powerful shoulder muscles flexed as Jackie and Jenny squirmed in his hold. The jacket ended at his waist and faded Levis fit snugly over his taut backside and down the long length of his legs.

Get a grip, she told herself firmly. *Stop ogling the man's rear and focus on the job—and the babies.*

"Have you got the key?"

Nick's question startled her and she realized he'd halted outside a room.

Feeling her cheeks heat and hoping he hadn't caught her staring at his backside, she quickly slid the key card through the lock slot and opened the door.

"After you." Nick held the door while she carried Jessie inside.

"Nice. Very nice." She halted at the foot of the queen-size bed and glanced around, taking in a round table with three chairs tucked into one corner near the draped window.

Nick swept the room with a quick, assessing gaze. "Yeah, not bad. The connecting room is ours too." He bent and carefully set Jackie on the carpeted floor, then Jenny. Straightening, he took another key card from his back pocket and crossed the room to open the door to the room on the side. "They're exactly the same," he said after briefly looking. He returned and halted next to Jackie, bending to remove a handful of bedspread from her mouth. "Hey," he said gently. "I'm not sure you should be chewing on that."

"She's probably hungry." Charlene set Jessie on her diaper-padded bottom next to Jackie, and handed both girls a small stuffed bear each. Both beamed up at her and Jackie instantly shoved a furry bear leg into her mouth. "Hmmm, make that she's *definitely* hungry."

"I'll bring up the bag with their food before the rest of the luggage. Anything else you need right away?"

"If you could bring up the diaper bag too, that would be great."

He nodded and left the room.

"Well, girls, let's see what we can do to make you comfortable." Charlene laughed when Jessie blew a raspberry before smiling beatifically. "Are you going to be the class clown?" she teased.

Jessie gurgled and tipped sideways before righting herself and reaching for Jackie's bear.

"Oh no you don't, kiddo." Charlene made sure each little girl had their own stuffed animal before calling the front desk. The clerk assured her he would arrange to have three high chairs from the restaurant sent to the room immediately. He also confirmed that Nick had requested three cribs during check-in and that someone would be delivering and setting them up within a half hour.

Satisfied that arrangements were under way, Charlene barely had time to replace the phone in its cradle before Nick returned with the box containing baby paraphernalia and two bags.

For the next two hours, neither she nor Nick had a moment to draw a deep breath. The high chairs were delivered while he was bringing in the luggage. Later, Charlene and Nick spooned food into little mouths, wiped chins and sticky fingers and tried to keep strained carrots from staining their own clothes.

Neither of them wanted to tackle eating dinner in the restaurant downstairs while accompanied by the triplets, so they ordered in. Nick insisted Charlene eat first, and she hurried to chew bites of surprisingly good pasta and chicken while he lay on the carpet, rolling rubber balls to the triplets. By the time Charlene's plate was empty, all three babies were yawning and rubbing their eyes.

The two adults switched places—Nick taking Charlene's chair to eat his steak, Jessie perched on his knee while Jackie played on the floor at his feet.

Charlene toted Jenny into the bathroom and popped her into the tub to scrub the smears of strained plums and carrots from her face and out of her hair.

By the time she had Jenny dried, freshly diapered and tucked into footed white pajamas patterned with little brown monkeys, Nick had finished eating.

"Hey, look at you," he said to Jenny. "What happened to the purple-and-orange face paint?"

Charlene laughed. "She even had it in her hair."

"I think they all do." Nick rubbed his hand over Jessie's black curls and grimaced. "Definitely sticky."

"I'm guessing that's the strained plums," Charlene said. She handed Jenny to him and lifted Jessie into her arms. "Will you watch her and Jackie while I put Jessie in the tub?"

"Sure—but I can bathe her if you'd like a break. I'm sure I can manage."

"No, I'm fine. Besides," she perched Jessie on her hip and started unbuttoning and unsnapping the baby's pants and knit shirt, "I'm already wet from being splashed by Jenny. One of us might as well stay dry."

Nicholas wished she hadn't pointed out that she'd been splashed with bathwater. He'd noticed the wet spots on her T-shirt and the way the damp cotton clung to her curves in interesting places. He was trying damned hard to ignore his body's reaction—and he was losing the battle.

"Uh, yeah. Okay, then. I'll keep these two occupied out here." He perched Jenny on his lap and she settled against him, her lashes half-lowered, apparently content to sit quietly. Nick bent his head, breathing in the scent of baby shampoo from her damp curls.

Something about the baby's warm weight resting trustingly in his arms and the smell of clean soap touched off an onslaught of unexpected emotion, followed quickly by a slam of grief that caught him off guard. The sound of splashing and gurgles from the bathroom, accompanied by Charlene's murmured reply, only heightened the pain in Nick's chest.

Stan and Amy must have fed and bathed the girls every night. Stan probably held Jenny just like this.

How was it possible that Stan and Amy were gone—and their children left alone? In what universe did any of this make sense?

It didn't—none of it, he thought. His arms tightened protectively around the baby.

He was the last person on earth who should be responsible for these kids; but since he was, he'd make damn sure they were cared for—and safe. As safe as he could make them.

Which means I have to rearrange my life.

He was a man who'd avoided the responsibilities of a wife and family until now. He enjoyed the freedom of being single and hadn't planned to change his status anytime soon; but now that surrogate fatherhood had been thrust on him, he would make the most of it.

While Charlene bathed Jessie and Jackie, Nick considered his schedule at work and the logistics of fitting three babies and a nanny into his house and life.

He was still considering the thorny subject when the triplets were asleep in their cribs and he had said good-night to Charlene before disappearing into the far bedroom. He lay awake, staring at the ceiling above his own bed while he formulated a plan.

He'd just drifted off to sleep when one of the babies cried. By the time he staggered into the room next door, all three of them were awake and crying. Charlene stood at one of the cribs, lifting the sobbing little girl into her arms.

"I'll take Jessie into your room to change her diaper and try to get her back to sleep. I think she's running a bit of a fever—probably because of the ear infection. Can you deal with the other two?"

"Sure," Nick mumbled. Charlene disappeared into her room. He patted the nearest baby on the back but she only cried louder. "Damn," he muttered. "Now what do I do?"

He picked her up and she burrowed her face into his shoulder, her wails undiminished. Feeling totally clueless, Nick jiggled her up and down, but the sobbing continued unabated. Willing to try anything, he grabbed her abandoned blanket from the crib mattress and handed it to her. She snatched it and clutched it in one hand, sucking on her thumb. She still cried but the sound diminished because her mouth was closed.

Which left him with the baby still standing in her crib, tears streaming down her face, her cries deafening.

Nick's head began to pound. He leaned over and

snagged the abandoned blanket, caught the little girl with one arm and lifted her to a seat on his hip. Then he lowered the two onto the empty bed, his back against the headboard. He managed to juggle both babies until he could cradle each of them against his chest, their security blankets clutched tightly in their hands. The first baby he'd picked up was crying with less volume, but the second one still made enough noise to wake the dead.

Vaguely remembering a comment his mother had made about singing her boys to sleep when they were little, Nick sang the only tune that came to mind. Bob Seger may not have intended his classic, "Rock And Roll Never Forgets" as a lullaby, but the lyrics seemed to strike a chord with the babies.

The loud sobs slowly abated. Nick felt the solid little bodies relax and gradually sink against his own. When the girls were limp and no longer crying, he tilted his head back to peer cautiously at them.

They were sound asleep.

Thank God. He eyed the cribs, trying to figure out how to lower each of the babies into their bed without waking one or both of them.

He drew a blank.

"Aw, hell," he muttered. He managed to shift one of the little girls onto the bed beside him before sliding lower in the bed until he lay flat. Then he grabbed a pillow, shoved it under his head and pulled the spread up over his legs and hips. "If you can't beat 'em, join 'em."

The sheets were still warm from Charlene's body,

and the scent of her perfume clung to the pillow, teasing his nostrils. He gritted his teeth and tried not to think about lying in her bed as he slid into sleep.

Nick woke the following morning with a kink in his neck and the sound of gleeful chortles accompanying thumps on his head from a tiny fist. He slitted his eyes open. He was nose-to-nose with a tiny face whose bright blue eyes sparkled with mischief below a mop of black curls.

He forced his eyes open farther just in time to see a second little girl as she wriggled out of his grasp and crawled toward the edge of the bed with determined speed. He grabbed a handful of her sleeper just in time to keep her from tumbling headfirst onto the floor.

The quick movement corresponded with a hard yank on his hair.

"Ow." He winced, pried little fingers away from his head and sat up. "You little imp." The tiny wrist bracelet told him this triplet was Jackie. "I'm gonna remember this," he told her.

She grinned, babbled nonsensically and began to crawl swiftly toward the end of the bed.

"Oh no you don't. Come back here." He hauled her back, then threw the spread back and stood, a wiggling little girl tucked beneath each arm. He lowered them each into a separate crib and grinned when they stood on tiptoes, reaching for him. "No way. You're trapped now and I'm not letting you out."

"Good morning."

He glanced over his shoulder. Charlene stood in the open doorway to the adjoining room, hair tousled, eyes sleepy. She was dressed in jeans and a pullover knit shirt, Jessie perched on one hip.

Nick was abruptly aware he was wearing only gray boxers.

"Morning." He gestured at the girls in their cribs. "I'll give you a hand with their breakfast as soon as I'm dressed. I'm going to jump in the shower."

She murmured an acknowledgment as he left the room.

Both adults were sleep-deprived and weary, but the triplets seemed little worse for their middle-of-the-night activity. By the time they were fed, dressed and strapped in their car seats, Nick was beginning to wonder if he should hire four or five nannies instead of one or two.

The trip from Amarillo south to Red Rock was just over five hundred and fifty miles. In normal circumstances, pretriplets, Nick could have driven the route in eight or nine hours with good road conditions and mild weather. But traveling with three babies on board drastically changed the time frame. After numerous stops to change diapers and feed the little girls, they finally reached his home in Red Rock in late afternoon of the second day.

Charlene stepped out of the SUV and stretched, easing muscles weary from sitting for too many hours. The SUV was parked in the driveway of a Spanish-style two-story stucco house on a quiet residential street in one of Red Rock's more affluent neighborhoods. She knew very little about this part of town; her previous apartment had been southeast, across the business district and blocks away.

In fact, she thought as she glanced up and down the broad street, with its large homes and neatly trimmed lawns, she didn't remember ever having been in this part of Red Rock before.

Good, she thought with satisfaction. Her belief that it would be unlikely she might run into Barry or his friends seemed to be accurate.

She turned back to the SUV and leaned inside to unhook Jessie from her seat belt.

"I called my housekeeper this morning," Nick told her as he unbuckled Jackie on the opposite side of the vehicle. "Melissa promised to come by and fill the fridge and pantry with food for the girls. She said she'd wait for the delivery van with the baby furniture too."

Surprised, Charlene's fingers stilled and she stopped unbuckling Jessie's seat belt to look at him across the width of the SUV's interior. "I didn't realize you'd made arrangements—but thank goodness you did."

Nick's gaze met hers and she felt her breath catch, helpless to stop her body's reaction to him.

"We were lucky last night," he said. "The hotel was prepared to accommodate babies. Trust me, there aren't any high chairs or cribs stored in my attic." He lifted Jackie free and grinned. "I'm not sure what we would have done with these three tonight if the store hadn't agreed to deliver and set up their beds today. The only thing I've got that comes close to cribs are a couple of large dog crates in the garage."

Charlene laughed, the sudden mental image of the three little girls sleeping in boxy carriers with gates was too preposterous.

"Exactly," Nick said dryly. He shifted Jackie onto his hip and unhooked Jenny from her seat.

He's much more comfortable with the babies after only a day. Charlene was impressed at how easily he'd managed to extricate Jenny from her seat while holding Jackie.

She quickly gathered the girls' blankets, stuffed animals and various toys from the floor mats where the girls had tossed them and finished unbuckling Jessie to lift her out of the car. She slung a loaded tote bag over her shoulder and bumped the car door closed with one hip.

"I'll unload the bags after we get the girls inside," Nick told her, gesturing her ahead of him to the walkway that curved across the lawn to the front entry. "Ring the doorbell," he said when they reached the door. "Melissa should be here—that's her car parked at the curb."

Charlene did as he asked and heard muted chimes from inside the house. Almost immediately the door opened.

"Hello—there you are." The woman in the doorway was small, her petite form sturdy in khaki pants, pullover white T-shirt and tennis shoes. Her dark hair was frosted with gray and her deep-brown eyes sparkled, animated behind tortoise-shell-framed glasses. "How was the trip?"

"Exhausting," Nick said bluntly. "Melissa, this is Charlene London. Charlene, this is Melissa Kennedy, my housekeeper. Charlene's going to take care of the girls, Melissa."

"Nice to meet you." Melissa's smile held friendly interest. Charlene's murmured response was lost as Jenny wriggled in Nick's arms, her little face screwing up into a prelude to full-blown tears. Nick stepped inside and handed Jackie to the housekeeper before he cuddled Jenny closer.

"Hey, what's wrong?" He carried the sobbing little girl down the hall.

Charlene followed him into the living room, Melissa bringing up the rear with Jackie.

As often happened with the three little girls, when one of them began crying, the other two soon followed. Charlene rubbed Jessie's back in soothing circles and slowly rocked her back and forth. She only cried harder. Melissa murmured to Jackie and gently patted her back, but Jackie's sobs increased until they matched her sisters' in volume.

"Jessie needs a diaper change." Charlene raised her voice to be heard over the combined cries of the three babies.

"Can you and Melissa handle them while I bring in the bags from the car?" Nick asked, looking faintly frazzled.

"Of course," Charlene responded with easy confidence.

Nick didn't look convinced but he didn't argue with her.

"Did the delivery crew set up the cribs, Melissa?" he asked.

"Yes, and the changing tables and dressers too. I put away the diapers and the other supplies in their room, and I had the men carry the high chairs into the kitchen," she replied.

"Good." Nick gently patted Jenny's back with one hand as he strode across the living room toward the stairway, located just inside the front door. "Let's get them upstairs and I'll bring in the diaper bags."

Charlene followed Nick and Melissa up the open stairway, with its wooden railing. The second-floor hallway branched to the right and left. Nick turned left and soon disappeared into the third room, Melissa and Jackie a step behind.

Charlene brought up the rear with Jessie, slowing to glance briefly into the first two rooms as she passed. One held a white, wrought-iron bed, the floor carpeted in light green Berber. The other was a bathroom, fitted in pale wooden cabinets with green marble tops.

The house was lovely but the sparse furnishings clearly stated that this was a bachelor's home. Downstairs in the living room, she'd noted a large plasma television mounted on one wall, with shelves of electronic equipment beneath. CD cases were piled in stacks on the shelves between stereo speakers. A low, oak coffee table sat in front of a dark-brown-leather sofa and a matching club chair and ottoman, angled next to the hearth of a river rock fireplace and chimney. There was no other furniture in the room, leaving an expanse of pale wooden floor gleaming in the late afternoon sunlight that poured through skylights and windows.

She'd glimpsed a dining room through an archway, but again, saw only the minimum of furniture in a table and chairs. She wondered how long Nick had lived in the house, since it appeared to be furnished with only essentials.

She carried Jessie into the bedroom and paused, feeling her eyes widen as she took in the room. It was large, with plenty of space for three white-painted cribs. Two dressers and changing tables matched the cottage-style cribs, and two rocking chairs with deep-rose seat cushions were tucked into a corner. Despite the number of pieces of furniture, the room didn't feel crowded.

Clearly, Nick hadn't skimped on furnishings here.

"I had the men put the third dresser, changing table and rocker in the empty bedroom down the hall," Melissa said to Nick. "I thought it would be too crowded if all of the furniture was in here."

"We might have to move two of the cribs into other rooms. If one of the girls cries, the other two chime in. Maybe they'd sleep better if we split them up." He looked at Charlene. "What do you think?"

"We could leave them together for tonight and see how they do. You can always move them tomorrow, if sharing a room doesn't work out."

Nick nodded decisively. "We'll try it." Gently, he

lowered the now quiet Jenny onto the carpet. "I'll go bring up their bags."

Charlene slipped the canvas tote off her shoulder and lowered it to the floor before kneeling and setting Jessie down next to it. She took a tissue from the bag and wiped the damp tears from Jessie's cheeks before handing the baby her blanket and a stuffed bear.

In Melissa's arms, Jackie's sobs had slowed to the occasional hiccup. She stretched out her arms and babbled imperiously.

Charlene wondered if she could use that combination of regal commands and pleas on Nick. Would he respond with hugs and kisses, as he did with the triplets?

She nearly groaned aloud.

The image of him rising from her bed at the motel, rumpled and sleepy, seemed to have permanently engraved itself on her brain. Try as she might, she couldn't forget how his big, powerful body had looked, clad only in gray boxers, as he'd walked across the room.

Jackie's chattering increased to shriek level and Charlene realized she had no idea how long she'd been standing still, staring unseeingly at the baby. She glanced quickly at Melissa, but the other woman was focused on Jackie, laughing as she jiggled her in her arms.

"I bet the queen of Hollywood divas, whoever she may be this week, doesn't make as much noise as this little girl," Melissa commented as she met

Charlene's gaze. The housekeeper's eyes twinkled with amusement.

Mentally sighing with relief that Melissa appeared oblivious to her distraction, Charlene shoved the memory of Nick's powerful thighs and broad chest into the back of her mind. She ordered the image to stay put—and desperately hoped it would obey.

Chapter Three

Jackie shrieked again and Charlene laughed out loud. "Yes, your royal highness," she said teasingly, retrieving the pink blanket with Jackie's name embroidered across one corner and passing it to Melissa.

"Isn't that clever?" Melissa said admiringly, as Jackie hugged the blanket and beamed at Charlene. "I wondered how Nick planned to tell one baby's things from another." She ran a fingertip gently over the bracelet on Jackie's wrist. "But everything has their names on it, including the little girls themselves."

"I thought their parents came up with a brilliant solution," Charlene agreed. "Though I assume they could tell their daughters apart."

Melissa's face sobered. "Such a terrible thing to have happened, isn't it? How awful to lose both parents at such a young age."

"Yes," Charlene agreed, her heart wrenching as she looked at Jessie and Jenny tugging on their stuffed bears. *So innocent—and thankfully, too young to grasp the enormity of their loss just now.*

Nick strode into the room, pulling two large rolling suitcases and carrying a backpack slung over one shoulder, all stuffed to overflowing with the triplets' clothing and toys. "I put your suitcase in the room across the hall," he told Charlene, shrugging the backpack off his shoulder.

"Thank you," she murmured, delighted to know the lovely room with the white wrought-iron bed and green carpet would be hers during her stay.

In the ensuing bustle of changing diapers and tucking away tiny clothing into dresser drawers, Charlene was too busy to dwell on the triplets' orphaned status.

Melissa was a godsend, helping with the girls as Charlene and Nick fed and bathed them, then tucked all three into bed. The adults returned to the living room and collapsed, Nick in the leather club chair, Charlene and Melissa on the comfortable sofa.

"They're wonderful," Melissa told Nick. "But oh, my goodness." She sighed, a gust of air stirring her normally smooth hair, where one of the triplets had rumpled and dampened it while the little girl splashed in her bath. "Talk about energy. What you two need to do is find a way to collect some of that for yourself. You're going to need it." She looked at Charlene. "Do they sleep through the night?"

"They did last night. I've got my fingers crossed, hoping we'll have another quiet ten hours or so."

"I hope they do too." Melissa pushed herself up off the sofa. "I'd better get home. Ed will be wondering what happened to me."

Nick started to shove up out of the chair but she waved him back. "No, no—don't get up. I can see myself out. You should take advantage of this moment of quiet. Who knows how long it will last?"

"Good point," Nick agreed, settling into the chair, the worn denim of his jeans going taut over muscled thighs as he stretched out his long legs. "We should make the most of this rare minute. It could be the last one of the night."

"Exactly." Melissa grinned at him, eyes twinkling, before she turned to Charlene. "I'll see you in the morning—about eight?"

"Eight works for me. I'm looking forward to it," Charlene replied with heartfelt warmth. After watching Melissa's efficient, comfortable and unflappable handling of the babies over the last couple of hours, Charlene was convinced the housekeeper was going to be an enormous help in caring for the triplets.

"Goodnight, then, you two. I hope you get some sleep. I left my purse and keys in the kitchen. I'll just collect them and let myself out the back," she said. She moved briskly across the living room but stopped in the doorway. "I forgot to tell you, Nick, I left Rufus with

Ed today so you could get the girls settled in before they meet him. I'll bring him back with me tomorrow."

"Good thinking," Nick told her. "Dealing with the triplets was chaotic. Adding an excited hundred-and-twenty-five-pound dog into the mix would have made it crazy."

Melissa chuckled and waved a quick good-night as she disappeared.

A moment later, the sound of her car engine reached the two in the living room.

"I take it you have a *big* dog?"

"Oh, yeah," Nick said dryly. "Rufus is a chocolate Lab. Thankfully, he's very mellow and loves kids, so he should be fine with the triplets."

"As long as he likes them, they'll probably think he's wonderful." Charlene yawned, suddenly exhausted. "I think I'll head upstairs." She unfolded her legs and stood, aware of aching muscles from the long car ride. "I could sleep for at least twelve hours straight. I've never understood how sitting in a car and doing nothing can make me tired."

"It was a long trip," Nicholas agreed, getting out of the chair. He rolled his shoulders and stretched. "Did Melissa show you where everything is— towels, coffee for tomorrow morning, et cetera?"

"Yes, thank you."

"If you need anything, just ask. If I don't already have it in the house, I'll get it." He eyed her, his gaze intent. "I'm damned grateful you agreed to take on the triplets, Charlene. I know it's not an easy job. There's no way I could do it by myself."

"You're doing very well for a man who's never had children of his own," she told him. "And I confess, I'm relieved Melissa will be helping. She's good with the girls and nothing seems to faze her."

"She's pretty unshakeable," Nick said. "I normally work long hours, and she keeps the house together and makes sure there are meals in the fridge."

"How long has she worked for you?" Charlene asked, curious.

"Since a few days after I moved to Red Rock. The employment agency sent over three women and I hired Melissa on the spot."

"Sounds like it was the right decision. Well…" She tugged her white cotton T-shirt into place, suddenly self-conscious. The room was abruptly too intimate in the lamplight and Nick loomed much too large, and much too male. "I'll see you in the morning."

"Sleep well. I have to go to the office for a meeting tomorrow, but I won't leave until Melissa arrives."

She nodded. "Good night."

His answering good-night was a low male rumble. Charlene looked back when she reached the stairway and found him staring after her, his expression brooding. She hurried up the stairs, faintly breathless from the impact of the brief moment her gaze had met his.

He's your employer, she reminded herself as she brushed her teeth in the white-and-green bathroom that opened off her bedroom, *stop lusting after him.*

Apparently, however, the emotional, hormonal part of her was in no mood to listen to the practical, rational command. She fell asleep and dreamed of making love with a man who looked very much like Nick Fortune.

Just as she stretched out her arms, her fingertips mere inches away from the bare chest of her dream lover, a loud wail yanked her awake.

Charlene sat bolt upright, disoriented as she stared in confusion at the dim outlines of bed and dresser in the strange room.

The sound of crying from the triplets' room abruptly scattered the lingering fog of sleep and she tossed back the bedcovers to hurry next door.

"Oh, sweetie," she soothed, lifting Jackie from her crib. "Sh." She patted the little back while the baby's sobs slowed to hiccups. "What's wrong?"

Jessie rolled over in her crib and sat up. In the third crib, Jenny pulled herself to her feet to clasp the rail. Jackie chose that moment to burst into sobs once more and, as if on cue, Jessie and Jenny's faces crumpled. They burst into tears as well.

The combined sound of their crying was deafening and impossible to ignore. Charlene wasn't surprised when Nick staggered into the room.

"What's wrong?" His voice was gravelly with sleep. He wore navy boxers, his broad chest and long legs bare.

Despite the earsplitting noise of three crying babies, Charlene still noticed that Nick looked as good undressed as he did in faded jeans and T-shirts.

"Jackie woke me, then her crying woke the other two." Charlene crossed to the changing table, gently rocking the still sobbing Jackie while she took a fresh diaper from the drawer. "I think she needs a diaper change. Can you pick up Jenny and Jessie— maybe rock them for a few minutes?"

"Sure." Nick shoved his fingers through his hair, further rumpling it, and lifted Jenny from her crib.

The low rumble of his voice as he murmured to the two babies was barely audible as Charlene quickly changed Jackie's diaper. By the time she snapped the little girl's footed sleeper and tossed the damp disposable nappy into the bin, their crying had subsided into silence. She tucked Jackie against her shoulder and turned, stopping abruptly.

Nick sat in the cushioned rocking chair, a little girl against each bare shoulder, their faces turned into the bend of his neck where shoulder met throat. His broad hands nearly covered each little back, fingers splayed to hold them securely. His hair was rumpled, his eyes sleepy.

Charlene didn't think she'd ever seen anything half as sexy as the big man protectively cradling the two sleeping babies. She felt her heart lurch.

Don't go there, she ordered herself. *Do not notice how sexy he is. Remember you swore to avoid men for at least six months after breaking up with Barry.* That was only two weeks ago.

She couldn't remember ever feeling this attracted to her ex-fiancé, but that didn't change the fact that she was determined to never, ever, get involved with her employer.

She moved softly across the room and eased into the empty rocking chair. Jackie stirred, lifting her head from Charlene's shoulder. Charlene quickly smoothed her hand over the baby's silky black curls, gently urging her to lay her head down once more, and set the rocker in motion. Within seconds, Jackie was relaxed, her compact little body feeling boneless where it lay against Charlene.

"Is she asleep?" Nick's murmur rasped, velvet over gravel.

"Yes," Charlene whispered. "What about your two?"

He tipped his head back to peer down at first one, then the other, of the two little girls. "They seem to be." He looked up at her. "Think it's safe to put them back in bed?"

"We can try. Let me put Jackie down and then I'll take one of yours." At his nod, Charlene stood and crossed to Jackie's crib, easing the sleeping baby down onto her back and pulling the light blanket over her before she returned to Nick.

"Which one do you want me to carry?" she whispered.

"Jenny." He leaned forward slightly.

Charlene bent closer to lift the sleeping baby, her hands brushing against his bare skin. He was warm, his skin sleek over the flex of muscles as he shifted to help transfer the little girl to her, and a shiver of awareness shook her. She was aware his head turned abruptly, could feel the intensity of his stare, but she wouldn't, couldn't, allow herself to meet his gaze. Instead, she cradled Jenny in her arms and turned away to carry the little girl to her crib, tucking her in and smoothing the blanket over her sleeping form. Behind her, she heard the soft sounds of Nick tucking Jessie into the third crib.

Nick followed her to the doorway, waiting in the hall as she paused to look back. The room was quiet—no movement visible in any of the three cribs to indicate a restless child.

"I think they're out for the count," Nick murmured behind her.

"Yes, I believe you're right," she whispered, before stepping into the hall and easing the door partially closed. "Let's hope they stay that way for the rest of the night." She gave him a fleeting glance. "Good night."

"Good night."

Once again, she felt his stare as she walked down the hall and into the safety of her room. She closed the door and collapsed against it, the panels cool against her shoulders, left bare by the narrow straps of her camisole pajama top.

There was no way she would ever become involved with her boss. She'd sworn a solemn oath after she'd learned about her father's affair with his secretary that had ultimately destroyed her parents' marriage. She'd never forgiven him, but for the first time, tonight she had an inkling as to what may have caused her father to stray. If he'd felt anything like the sizzling heat that swamped her every time she got close to Nick Fortune, then maybe, just maybe, she should stop being so angry at him. Maybe he'd literally been unable to help himself.

Or not, she thought, still not completely convinced.

But in any event, she had to find a way to insulate herself against the powerful attraction she felt. Especially since it appeared Nick didn't have to do anything, or even say anything, to make her nerves sizzle and her body heat up.

Apparently, he just needed to breathe in her presence.

Groaning, she climbed back into bed and pulled the sheet and blanket over her head.

The triplets were still fast asleep in their cribs upstairs when Charlene tiptoed down the stairs and into the kitchen just before eight the following morning.

Nick glanced over his shoulder and took down another mug from the open cupboard. "Morning," he said. "Coffee's nearly done."

Charlene breathed in the rich scent filling the kitchen and nearly groaned. "Bless you."

Nick's grin flashed, his eyes lit with amusement. He poured the rich brew into their mugs at the same moment that a knock sounded on the back door.

"That'll be Melissa," Nick told Charlene. He grabbed his computer case and crossed the kitchen to pull open the door.

A huge chocolate Labrador retriever leaped over the threshold and planted his paws on Nick's shoulders, whining with excitement, his tail whipping back and forth.

"Ouch." Melissa stepped inside, moving sideways

to avoid getting hit. "That tail of yours is a lethal weapon, Rufus." She waved her hand at the travel coffee mug and leather case in Nick's left hand. "On your way out to work, boss?"

"Yeah." Nick rubbed Rufus's ears. "That's enough. Down, boy." The Lab dropped back onto four paws but continued to wag his tail, pink tongue lolling as he stared adoringly up at Nick. "I'll check with the employment agency today," Nick said, looking over his shoulder at Charlene, "and find out if they've lined up applicants for a second nanny."

"I'll keep my fingers crossed that they have—then maybe we both can start getting more sleep."

Nick grinned, his eyes lit with rueful amusement as his mouth curved upward to reveal a flash of white teeth. Charlene suspected she was staring at him like a hopelessly lovestruck teenager, but she couldn't bring herself to look away.

No man should be that gorgeous.

"I'll tell them we're staggering from sleep deprivation. Maybe they'll take pity on us," he said.

"We can only hope," Charlene said, tearing her gaze away from his smile. Unfortunately, she was immediately snagged by his glossy black hair, thick-lashed brown eyes, tanned skin with a faint beard shadow despite the early hour, handsome features... Were all the Fortune men this blessed by nature? she wondered. If so, heaven help the women who caught their attention—because females didn't stand a chance against all that powerful, charming, handsome male virility. Perhaps she was fortunate that he was her boss and thus off-limits, not to mention he was also clearly far more sophisticated than she. Never mind the fact that he was also not interested in her. Because if he ever turned that undeniable charm on her, she'd give in without a whimper.

It's a pitiful thing when a woman has *no* resistance to a man, she realized with wry acknowledgment.

"So long, boss," Melissa's voice yanked Charlene out of her thoughts. "Have a good day."

"Good luck with the triplets." Nick bent to give Rufus's silky ears one last rub before disappearing through the door.

Charlene echoed Melissa's goodbye before pouring herself another mug of coffee. "The coffee's fresh," she told Melissa. "Want some?"

"Sure, why not." Melissa slid onto a stool at the counter.

Charlene handed her a steaming cup and took a seat opposite her.

"Are the babies still asleep?" Melissa asked.

"Yes." Charlene glanced at the digital clock on the microwave. "They're sleeping in, probably because they were awake several times last night."

"I was telling my Ed about the triplets just this morning—" Melissa began.

Whatever she was about to say was lost as someone rapped sharply on the back door.

Charlene looked inquiringly at Melissa.

"That's probably LouAnn," Melissa said as she left the counter and crossed the room.

Charlene barely had time to wonder who LouAnn

was before Melissa pulled open the door. She felt her eyes widen.

"Good morning, Melissa." The throaty rasp seemed incongruous, coming as it did from a woman who Charlene guessed weighed at best a hundred pounds, maybe a hundred and ten at the most.

"Hi, LouAnn." Melissa gestured her inside. "We're just having coffee. Want some?"

"Of course." LouAnn followed Melissa to the counter, her bright blue gaze full of curiosity and fixed on Charlene. "And who are you, dearie?"

"I'm Charlene, the nanny." Charlene tried not to stare, but the silver-haired woman's attire was eye-popping. She wore a turquoise T-shirt with a bucking horse and rider picked out in silver rhinestones. The black leggings below the T-shirt clung to her nonexistent curves and hot-pink, high-top tennis shoes covered her feet. Skinny arms poked out of the loose short sleeves of the shirt, and both hands boasted jewelry that dazzled. Charlene was pretty sure the huge diamond on her left hand was real, and more than likely, so was the sapphire on her right. Not to mention the large diamond studs that glittered in her earlobes. She was tan, toned and exuded energy that fairly vibrated the air around her pixie frame.

"Nanny?" LouAnn's penciled eyebrows shot toward the permed silver curls of her immaculate, short hairdo. "Why does Nick need a nanny?"

"Have a seat, LouAnn, and we'll fill you in." Melissa pulled out a chair next to hers and across the island's countertop from Charlene. "Charlene, this is Nick's neighbor, LouAnn Harris."

"Pleased to meetcha." LouAnn hopped onto the tall chair, crossed her legs and beamed at Charlene. "You might as well know you're likely to see a lot of me. I'm a widow. I live alone and my son and daughter live too far away to visit me often, so I tend to get bored. I was delighted when Nick moved in here and hired Melissa—we've known each other for at least twenty years. My, you're young, aren't you?"

"Uh, well…" Charlene looked at Melissa for guidance. The housekeeper grinned, her eyes twinkling. Clearly, she wasn't bothered by the neighbor's bluntness. "I suppose I am, sort of," Charlene replied, taking her cue from Melissa.

LouAnn snorted. "No 'sort of' about it, honey. Compared to me, you're a child. But then, I'm seventy-six, so most everyone *is* younger." She sipped her coffee. "I have to get me a coffeemaker like Nick's. Your coffee is always better than mine, Melissa."

"That might be because I grind the beans. Nick has them sent from the coffee shop he used to go to in L.A.," Melissa explained to Charlene.

"I thought it was the coffeemaker." LouAnn leaned forward and lowered her voice to a raspy whisper. "It looks like it belongs on a space ship."

Charlene laughed, charmed by LouAnn's warm camaraderie.

LouAnn grinned at her, winked, and turned back to Melissa. "Now, tell me why Nick needs a nanny.

I thought he was a confirmed bachelor with no interest in kids."

"He is—and he doesn't, or didn't, pay attention to children," Melissa agreed. "At least, he had no interest in children until recently. It's a sad story, really."

When she finished relaying a condensed version of the situation, LouAnn clucked in sympathy. "How terrible for those poor little girls. And how lucky for them—and Nick—that you were willing to step in and help," she added, reaching across the marble countertop to pat Charlene's hand.

"It was fate," Melissa said firmly. "That's what I think."

"Three little ones—all the same age." LouAnn shook her head. "How are you all coping?"

"Except for a serious lack of sleep, fairly well, I think." Charlene looked at Melissa. "Sometimes it's chaos, of course, but the girls seem to be doing okay. Jessie has an ear infection at the moment, so she's a little cranky. But by and large, they're very sweet little girls."

"I can't wait to see them. How old are they?"

"They're a year—uh-oh." The sound of one of the girls, chattering away upstairs floated down the stairway and into the kitchen. "I think you're about to meet the dynamic trio." Charlene slipped off her chair and headed for the door.

"I'm coming up with you," LouAnn announced, joining Charlene.

Melissa brought up the rear as the three women left the kitchen.

* * *

Nick had a long list of priorities for the day, but as he backed his Porsche out of the garage and drove away, he wasn't focusing on the work waiting for him at the Fortune Foundation. Instead, he was distracted by the memory of Charlene coping with the babies in the middle of the night.

The picture of her in the bedroom, lit only by the glow of a night-light, was seared in his memory. Her auburn hair had been rumpled from sleep, her long legs covered in soft-looking, blue-and-white pajama bottoms. Jackie had clutched the neckline of the brief little white tank top Charlene wore, pulling it down to reveal the upper curve of her breasts.

Even half-asleep, he'd been damn sure she wasn't wearing anything under that top. He felt like a dog for looking, and hoped she hadn't noticed.

He'd known having the beautiful redhead living in his house was bound to cause difficult moments, but he hadn't been prepared to be blindsided by a half-naked woman when he was barely awake.

Which was stupid of me, he thought with disgust. *She's living in my house. I knew she'd be getting out of bed if one of the triplets woke during the night.*

And as long as he was being brutally honest, he had to admit the pajamas she wore hadn't come close to being blatantly suggestive. Nevertheless, Charlene's simple pajama bottoms and tank top would stop traffic on an L.A. freeway.

Maybe he wouldn't have felt as if he'd been hit

by lightning when he saw her in those pajamas if she were a woman with fewer curves.

Or maybe, he thought with self-derision, *if she'd been wearing a sack I'd still have been interested.*

He knew he was completely out of line. He just didn't know how to turn off his body's response to her. Not only was she his employee, she was too damned young for him. His office assistant had telephoned with results of a preemployment background check before he'd left his hotel to drive to the triplets' foster home. The report not only confirmed Charlene had a spotless employment record, it also told him she'd graduated from college only three years earlier.

A brief mental calculation told him that if she'd gone to college immediately after high school, then graduated after four or five years before working for three more years, she most likely was twenty-five or twenty-six years old.

And he was thirty-seven. Too old for her.

Unfortunately, his libido didn't appear to be paying attention to the math.

He'd reached the office while he'd been preoccupied with the situation at home, and swung the Porsche into a parking slot. He left the car and headed for his office, determined to put thoughts of the curvy redhead at home, busy with his new instant family, out of his mind.

He quickly scanned the pink message slips the receptionist had handed him and tossed the stack on his desktop. He rang his brother Darr while he plugged in his laptop and arranged to meet him for lunch at their favorite diner, SusieMae's. Then he closed his office door and tackled an inbox filled with documents and files.

Nick gave the waitress his and Darr's usual lunch order and she bustled off. SusieMae's Café was crowded, but he had a clear view of the door, and saw his brother enter.

Darr swept the comfortable interior with a quick glance, nodding at acquaintances as he crossed the room and slid into the booth across from Nick.

"Where have you been?" he demanded without preamble. "I left two messages on your machine. You never called back."

"You didn't say it was an emergency." Nick shrugged out of his jacket and eyed his brother across the width of the scarred tabletop. "Was it?"

"Not exactly. I wanted to know if you'd talked to Dad or J.R. lately."

"I haven't." Nick took a drink of water. "Why?"

"Because I called and neither one answered. Come to think of it," Darr frowned at Nick, "none of you called me back."

Nick grinned. "Probably because we all assumed you were too busy with Bethany to care if we called you or not."

"Huh," Darr grumbled.

Nick noticed his younger brother didn't deny the charge.

"How's Bethany doing?" he asked. He felt distinctly protective toward the petite, pregnant blonde, especially since Darr was in love with her. When the two married, she'd become Nick's sister-in-law. As far as he was concerned, Bethany Burdett was a welcome addition to their all-male family.

"Good." Darr leaned back to let their waitress set plates and coffee mugs on the tabletop in front of them. "She's good."

Nick didn't miss the softening of his brother's face. He was glad Darr had found a good woman. Bethany made him happy, and he seemed content in a way Nick hadn't seen before.

"You didn't answer my question, where have you been?"

Nick waited until the waitress left before he spoke. "I made a trip to Amarillo. I've been pretty busy since I got back."

"Yeah? What were you doing in Amarillo?" Darr took a bite of his sandwich, eyeing Nick over the top of a double-decker bacon-and-tomato on wheat.

"I picked up Stan's kids." Nick saw Darr's eyes widen. "Three of them," he added, smiling slightly at the shock on his brother's face. "They're all girls— only a year old. Triplets."

Darr choked, set down his sandwich, grabbed his coffee and washed down the bite in record time. "What the hell? Why? What happened?"

Nick lost any amusement he'd felt at his brother's dumfounded expression. "He and Amy were in a car accident—neither one of them made it out alive." Saying the words aloud didn't make the truth any less surreal.

The shock on Darr's face made it clear he was just as stunned as Nick had been at first hearing the news.

"Both of them?" He shook his head in disbelief when Nick nodded. "They were so young. You and Stan are the same age, right?"

Again, Nick nodded. "And Amy was a year younger."

"And you have custody of their babies?" Darr queried,

"Yeah."

"Why?"

"Because Stan's will named me guardian if Amy's sister Lana couldn't take them." Nick took a drink of coffee, hoping to erase the lump of emotion in his throat. He still hadn't come to terms with the abruptness with which Stan and Amy had disappeared from the world. "So they're with me until the attorney locates Lana."

"Where is she?"

"No one knows." Nick stared broodingly at his plate, holding a sandwich and chips. "She and her husband work in Africa and Amy seems to have lost track of them a few months ago."

"Damn." Darr eyed him. "Who's taking care of the kids while you work?"

"I hired a nanny," Nick replied. "And Melissa's working longer hours while I'm at the Foundation during the day."

Darr stared at him. Nick took a bite of his sandwich.

"And?" Darr prompted when Nick didn't elaborate.

"And what?"

"Don't give me that. You're stalling. What else aren't you telling me?"

"The nanny I hired works full-time. Her name is Charlene. She's a redhead and she's great with the triplets."

Darr lowered his coffee mug to the table without taking his gaze from Nick's face. "She's a babe, isn't she."

It wasn't a question. Darr knew him too well to be fooled.

"Yeah. She is." Nick shoved another bite of sandwich into his mouth.

"Full-time," Darr said consideringly. "What hours does she work?"

"She's pretty much on call twenty-four hours a day."

"So…she's living at your house?"

"Yeah."

"Sleeping down the hall from you?"

Nick nodded, saw the glint appear in Darr's eyes and bristled. "Yes, *down the hall.* She has her own bedroom. What the hell did you think, that she was sharing mine?"

Darr shrugged. "It did cross my mind. Face it, Nick, you've never been slow with the ladies. You said she's pretty—and she's living in your house…." He spread his hands. "Sounds like a no-brainer to me."

"Well, it's not," Nick snarled, restraining an urge to wrap his hands around his brother's neck and choke that grin off his face. "She works for me. Have you heard of sexual harassment? She's off-limits."

"Too bad." Darr lifted his coffee mug and drank.

"So," he said, setting the mug down and picking up his sandwich, "just how good-looking is Charlene?"

Too beautiful. Nick bit back the words and shrugged. "Beautiful."

"On a scale of one to ten?"

"She's a fifteen."

Darr's eyes widened. "Damn."

"And she's too young," Nick continued.

"How young?"

"She's twenty-five."

"Thank God." Darr pretended to wipe sweat off his brow in relief. "I thought you were going to tell me she's underage and jailbait."

"Might as well be," Nick growled. "She's twelve years younger than me. That's too damned young."

Darr pursed his lips. "Let me see if I've got this straight. You're cranky because you've got a nanny you can't make a move on because you're her boss and she's younger than you."

"Yeah, pretty much," Nick conceded.

Darr grinned. "Maybe you should fire her. Then you can date her."

"I can't fire her—and I don't want to," Nick ground out. "She's good at her job. If she wasn't helping me take care of the girls, I'd be screwed."

"So hire someone else—and then fire her."

"Yeah, like she's likely to go out with me after I've fired her." Nick rubbed his eyes. They felt as if there was a pound of sand in each of them. If he didn't get some sleep soon, he'd need more than the saline eyedrops he'd been using in a vain attempt to solve the problem. "There's no solution that's work-able. Believe me, I've considered all the angles."

"Where there's a will, there's a way."

"Stop being so damned cheerful," Nick growled.

"Aren't you the one who told me there's always another girl just around the corner? Wait a week and there'll be another corner, another girl. If things don't work out with the redhead, why do you care?"

Because I've never met anyone quite like her.

Nick didn't want to tell Darr that Charlene was unique. He was having a hard enough time accept-ing that he'd met a woman who broke all the rules he'd spent thirty-seven years setting.

"Maybe you're right," he said with a slight shrug, neither agreeing nor disagreeing. "Have you heard anything new about the note Patrick got at the New Year's Eve party? Or about the ones Dad and Cindy received?"

"No." Darr didn't appear thrown by Nick's abrupt change of subject. "That's one of the reasons I wanted to talk to Dad and J.R.—to ask if they've learned anything more."

The Fortune family had gone through a series of mysterious events over the last few months, starting with the cryptic note left in Patrick Fortune's jacket pocket during a New Year's Eve party. The strange message—"One of the Fortunes is not who you think"—baffled the family, even more so when they learned the same message had been left anony-mously with Cindy Fortune and William, Nick and Darr's father.

Patrick had called a family conference at Lily Fortune's home on the Double Crown Ranch in February, on the very day Red Rock had been hit with a freak snowstorm.

Darr hadn't been present at the gathering, since he'd been snowed-in with Bethany in her little house. But Nick had brought him up to speed on everything that happened, including the family's assumption the notes were the precursor to a blackmail demand. So far, however, no such demand had been made. But two subsequent fires—one that burned down the local Red Restaurant, and a second that destroyed a barn at the Double Crown—were suspicious. And potentially connected to the mysterious and vaguely threatening notes.

"Let me know if you reach Dad and J.R.," Nick said. "Meanwhile, I had a message from Ross Fortune when I got back to the office today. We set up a meeting to discuss the notes and fires. Has he contacted you?" Nick and Darr's cousin was a private investigator with an agency in San Antonio. His mother, Cindy, had convinced the family they should hire him to check into the cryptic threats.

"Not yet," Darr said, "but I heard he's in town. The Chief said he called and asked for copies of the department's report on the fire at Red." Darr pushed his empty plate aside and leaned his elbows on the tabletop, his voice lowering. "This isn't for public knowledge, but I'm sure my boss agrees with us— he has serious reservations as to whether the fire was accidental."

"What about the barn that burned at the Double Crown?"

"He didn't want to talk about that one—I suspect he believes I'm too close to the subject, since it happened on Lily's ranch."

"Do you have a gut feeling as to his opinion?"

"Yeah. I'm convinced he believes the Double Crown fire wasn't an accident, either."

"I hope to hell Ross's investigation gets some answers," Nick said grimly. "You or someone else could have died in those fires."

"Bethany damn near did," Darr said darkly, his features hardening. "She was barely conscious when I found her on the bathroom floor at the restaurant. She could have died of smoke inhalation."

"We have to find out who's behind these threats to the family before someone loses their life," Nick said. "I hope Ross is good at his job."

"When are you talking to him?"

"Tomorrow afternoon at one." Nick glanced at his watch. "I have a meeting in a half hour. Gotta get back to the office."

Darr nodded and both men dropped money on top of the check.

"Thanks, guys," their waitress called after them as they left the booth and headed for the exit.

Nick shrugged into his jacket as he stepped outside, a brisk breeze cooling the air, although the sun beamed down, warm against his face.

"Let me know what Ross has to say tomorrow," Darr said, pausing on the sidewalk. "I have the day off, but I'm not sure what Bethany's plans are or if I'll be home, so call my cell phone."

"Sure." Nick stepped off the curb. "Tell Bethany hello from me."

"Will do." Darr headed down the block to his vehicle.

Nick climbed into his Porsche, the powerful engine turning over with a throaty, muted roar when he twisted the key. The low-slung car had only two seats—room for the driver and one passenger.

"Too small," Nick murmured as he backed out of the slot. "I need to get an SUV." Or a minivan. He shuddered. He didn't think he could bring himself to drive a minivan—even for the triplets. Minivans were mommy cars. For a guy who loved fast cars and powerful engines, a minivan was a step too far, vehicle-wise.

He made a mental note to go SUV shopping on his lunch hour tomorrow. Charlene could use it to drive the babies during the week and he'd use it on the weekends if he needed to take the little girls anywhere.

If anyone had told him two weeks ago that he'd be contemplating buying a vehicle to transport babies, he would have laughed at the sheer insanity of the idea.

He didn't do kids. Never had. And kids hadn't been part of his plans for the future.

There was some kind of cosmic karma at work here. Nick couldn't help but wonder what fate planned to hit him with next.

Chapter Four

Nick returned to the office, where he forced himself to concentrate on meetings. By the time he reached home that evening, he'd almost convinced himself he'd overreacted that morning.

Surely he'd overestimated the power of his attraction to Charlene.

The neighborhood was quiet, the street lamps casting pools of light in the early darkness when he slotted the car into the garage and got out, tapping the panel next to the inner door to close the garage door smoothly behind him. He unlocked the door leading from the garage into the utility room and passed through, stopping abruptly in the open doorway to the kitchen when he saw Charlene. She stood at the stove across the room, her back to him as she poured steaming water from the stainless steel teakettle into a mug. A box of tea sat on the counter next to the cup. Her hair was caught up in a ponytail, leaving her nape bare above a short-sleeved green T-shirt tucked into the waistband of faded jeans. She wore thick black socks and she looked comfortable and relaxed, as if the kitchen were her own.

Coming home after a long day at work and finding a pretty woman in my kitchen is kind of nice.

The thought surprised him. He'd never really understood married friends when they insisted that walking into a house that wasn't empty was one of the great things about being married. He liked his privacy and didn't mind living alone. In fact, he thoroughly appreciated the solitude of his quiet house after a day spent in meetings.

But finding Charlene in his kitchen, clearly comfortable and making herself at home, felt good.

Of course, he thought wryly, *maybe I'd feel differently if she was a girlfriend with marriage on her mind and not the nanny.* Maybe her employee status erased the natural wariness of a bachelor when confronted with an unmarried, attractive woman puttering in his kitchen.

Whatever's going on here, Nick thought, *I'm definitely glad to see her.*

Before he could say hello, Rufus bounded in from the living room, his nails clicking against the tile floor. Woofing happily, he charged. Nick quickly lowered his leather computer bag to the tile and braced himself. The big dog skidded to a halt, reared onto his back legs, planted his front paws on Nick's shoulders and tried to lick his face.

"Hey, stop that." Nick caught Rufus's head in his palms and rubbed his ears.

"Hi." Charlene looked over her shoulder at him. She set the kettle on the range and carried her mug to the island where a notebook lay open beside her laptop computer. "I thought I heard your car pull into the garage. How was your day?"

"Busy," he said, releasing Rufus and bending to pick up his computer bag. The big dog followed Nick to the island and flopped down next to Charlene's chair. "How was yours?"

"Busy."

He laughed at her dry, one-word response. "Yeah, I bet it was. How did it go with the girls?"

"Fine." Charlene spooned sugar into her tea and stirred. "Jackie bonked her chin on a chair rung and has a new little bruise. Jessie smeared oatmeal in her hair and had to have a second bath this morning barely an hour after her first one. And Jenny…" She paused, her eyes narrowing in thought. "Come to think of it, Jenny had a fairly quiet day."

"That doesn't sound possible."

"I know," she laughed. "But she doesn't seem ill, so I'm happy—but surprised—to report that although I've only known them for three days, there's a possibility that maybe one of them has an uneventful day on occasion."

"Well, that's a relief."

"Did you talk to the employment agency today?"

"Yeah, they might have three candidates for me to interview soon. They're running background checks and verifying references for each of the women." Nick turned on the tap and washed his hands, turning to lean against the counter as he dried them. "What did Melissa make for dinner?"

"Lasagne, french bread and salad—she left a plate for you in the fridge and the bread is in the pantry." Charlene set down her mug and shifted to stand.

Nick waved her back. "Stay where you are, I'll get it." The stainless steel, double-door refrigerator was only a step away. He located the plate and salad bowl, took a bottle of dressing from the inner-door shelf and let the door swing closed behind him as he walked back to the counter. He peeled the plastic wrap off the lasagne and slid it into the microwave to heat, tapping the timer before closing the door.

"What do you want to drink?"

He glanced around to see Charlene at the fridge, glass in hand.

"Ice water sounds good, thanks."

He heard the clink of ice and the splash of water behind him as he walked to the island and pulled out one of the low-backed stools. The microwave pinged just as he finished pouring vinegar and oil dressing on his salad and he returned to the counter, grabbing a knife and fork from the cutlery drawer. Charlene set his glass of water down next to his salad bowl and returned to her seat as he carried his steaming plate back to the island. He sat across from Charlene and folded his shirt cuffs back, loosening and tugging off his tie.

"Tell me about the triplets," he said. "How did Melissa survive the day?"

"She said she's going to cancel her gym membership. Evidently, lifting and carrying three babies for eight hours is more fun than weight lifting with her trainer." Charlene laughed. "Seriously, she's great with them, and they seem to like her as much as she likes them."

"I thought they would," Nick commented. "She's good with Rufus, and dealing with him seems to be a lot like having a toddler in the house—he makes messes, demands food regularly, requires massive amounts of attention and sometimes wakes me up in the middle of the night."

"So, what you're saying," Charlene said dryly, arching one eyebrow as she eyed him, "is that three little girls can cause as much havoc as a hundred-and-twenty-five-pound dog?"

"Pretty much," Nick agreed, grinning as she shook her head and frowned at him. The effect was ruined by the small smile that tugged her lips upward at the corners. "As a matter of fact, I can pick him up. I doubt I could juggle all three of the girls at the same time."

"You could, if you had a baby carrier," she said promptly.

"What's a baby carrier?"

"It's sort of a canvas backpack that an adult wears over their shoulders. The child is buckled into it so you can carry them on your chest or your back. Some are made for younger babies, but you can also get one to use for toddlers."

"Ah!" he said, nodding. "Remind me to get one of those. Then, if either of us ever has to take all three of the girls somewhere alone, we won't risk dropping one of them."

"That sounds like an excellent plan," Charlene agreed. "I met your neighbor LouAnn today."

"Did you?" Nick grinned and lifted an eyebrow. "What did you think of her?"

"She's a very interesting woman."

He laughed outright. "Got that right. She's a character. I hope I have that much energy when I'm seventy-something."

"Me too," Charlene agreed, smiling as she remembered LouAnn playing on the floor with the triplets. "She's wonderful with the babies. I'm not sure who had more fun playing peekaboo, her or the girls."

Nick chuckled, the sound sending shivers of awareness through Charlene's midsection. As he ate, they discussed the wisdom of keeping all three girls in the same bedroom.

Charlene sipped her tea, staring with fascination as Nick tipped his head back slightly and drank from the water glass. He'd unbuttoned the top two buttons of his shirt when he removed his tie earlier, and the strong, tanned muscles of his throat moved rhythmically as he swallowed. There was something oddly intimate about sitting in the cozy kitchen with him as he ate and they discussed his children.

"…What do you think?"

"Hmm?" She realized with a start that he'd been speaking while she'd stared at him, mesmerized, and felt embarrassed heat flood her cheeks. "I'm sorry, I didn't catch that. What do I think about…?"

His expression was quizzical. She suspected he noticed her pink cheeks, but she was determined not to become flustered. So she met his gaze with what she hoped was a serene look.

"I asked if you thought it was a good idea to give the girls a week or so together before we decide if they need to sleep in separate bedrooms."

"I think it makes sense to see whether they continue to wake each other, as they did last night." Charlene didn't want to remember the intimacy of the babies' darkened bedroom and the mental image of Nick wearing navy boxers and nothing else. Resolutely, she focused on the other bedrooms she'd seen during the tour of the house Melissa had given her that afternoon. "There's certainly plenty of room if you decide to have them sleep apart. Do you know if their parents had their cribs in separate bedrooms or if they all slept in the same room?"

Nick paused, his expression arrested. "The foster mother had the beds in two small bedrooms but I never thought to ask what the arrangements were at Stan and Amy's." He put down his fork with a thunk. "I should have asked," he said with disgust. "It never even occurred to me."

"If you have a phone number, I can try to reach her tomorrow," Charlene offered, touched by the sheer frustration on his face as he thrust his fingers through his hair and raked it back off his forehead.

"I'd appreciate that. I have her contact information in my desk in the den. Remind me to look it up before I leave for the office in the morning, will you?"

"Of course." Charlene sipped her tea and considered what she knew about the triplets' situation while Nick ate the last few bites of his lasagne. "Did the attorney have any estimate as to how long it might take to locate the babies' aunt?"

"No." Nick rose to carry his empty china and dirty cutlery to the sink. He turned on the tap. "He asked me to let him know if I remembered anything Stan or Amy may have said that would help find her. So far, all I've come up with is going through the photographs."

"Photographs? Does the investigator need a picture?"

"No, he has one." Nick slotted his rinsed dishes and utensils into the rack of the dishwasher and closed the door. "But Amy loved taking photographs—so did Stan—and Amy almost always jotted little notes on the back of the pictures. I'm sure some of the holiday photos they sent included her sister. I'm hoping there might be something in one of Amy's notes that will help locate Lana."

"That's a great idea," Charlene said, encouraged at the possibility of finding a clue.

"I hope it's a productive one, but who knows whether I'll learn anything new." He shrugged. "Still, it's one place we haven't looked yet, and given how little information the investigator has, any small piece might make a difference. When I moved in, I shoved the photo boxes into the back of a closet upstairs. I thought I'd bring one downstairs tomorrow night and start looking."

"I'd be glad to help you search through them," she offered.

"Thanks, but I should warn you, I've never organized the pictures. All the photos I have are tossed in a couple of boxes, and the ones from Stan and Amy are mixed in with all the rest. There might be hundreds of pictures to look at. My mom divided family photos a few years ago and gave me a carton full."

"I'll still volunteer," she said. "Did the attorney search the triplets' house for an address book? I keep a notebook with family and friends' addresses and phone numbers in a drawer by the phone. And in a computer file too," she added as an afterthought.

"Sanchez and the investigator both checked Amy's home computer but didn't find anything helpful. They also looked for an address book at the house," Nick said. "They didn't find one. Whether she carried one with her is unknown because they didn't find her purse at the accident scene. They're assuming it was probably lost or destroyed, if she even had it with her."

"What about old letters from her sister? Didn't Amy keep correspondence?"

"Yes, but the last letter Amy received from Lana was several months ago—just after Thanksgiving. The investigator tried contacting her using the phone number at that residence, but she's no longer living there. The landlord didn't have any forwarding information."

"So, what will he do now? Surely she just didn't disappear?"

"I'm guessing the agency will send someone to Africa to interview the landlord in person, talk to her former employer, et cetera. It's hard to investigate someone's whereabouts from halfway around the world—on another continent," Nick said grimly.

"Yes, I'm sure it is. Who knew it could be so difficult to locate someone?" she murmured. "This is a real wake-up call for me. I should think about what personal files and paperwork to organize in the remote chance I might suddenly disappear. I've never given any thought to the subject before now."

"Most people don't," Nick said, a slightly gravelly edge to his deep voice.

"Of course," she agreed, her tone softening. "It must have been a shock to get that phone call. Had you known each other a long time?"

"Since college." Nick's expression shuttered.

Charlene sensed his withdrawal. His expression didn't invite further questions. Without further comment, she logged off her computer and closed it before picking up her mug and walking to the sink.

"It's late. I think I'll try to get some rest while the triplets are all asleep."

"Not a bad idea." Nick yawned. "I need to let Rufus outside before I come up."

"Good night."

He murmured a response and Charlene left the room. She heard the click of a latch behind her and paused, glancing back. Nick was turned away from her as he held the door open for Rufus. The big dog trotted through and Nick followed, his tall frame silhouetted against the darkness by the kitchen light spilling through the open door.

She was struck by how very alone he looked, standing in the shaft of golden light, facing the black night, before she turned away and climbed the stairs.

He's your boss, she reminded herself firmly. *He's also older, more experienced. There is absolutely no reason for you to assume he's lonely. He's charming and probably wealthy, given his family ties, and no doubt has a little black book filled with the phone numbers of numerous women who'd be happy to keep him company.*

Fortunately, she didn't lie awake thinking about Nick. Being wakened by the triplets several times the night before, combined with her long day, made her tired enough to fall asleep almost the moment her head hit the pillow.

Unfortunately, Charlene wasn't allowed to remain asleep for long.

The first cry woke her just after 1:00 a.m. She tossed back the covers and fumbled for her slippers with her bare toes but couldn't find them. Giving up the search, she hurried across the hall to the triplets' room.

Jessie was standing up in her crib, holding on to the railing with one hand, the other clasping her beloved blanket. Although the room was lit by only the dim glow from the plug-in Winnie The Pooh night-light, Charlene could see the tears overflow and trickle down Jessie's flushed cheeks.

"Sh, sweetie," Charlene murmured, crossing the room and lifting the little girl into her arms. "What's wrong?"

Jessie burrowed her face against Charlene's neck. The heat coming from the little body was palpable.

"You're running a temperature," Charlene murmured, realizing the ear infection was no doubt responsible for the rise in body heat. Jackie and Jenny appeared to be sound asleep. Charlene sent up a quick prayer that they would remain so as she quickly carried Jessie out of the bedroom and into the room next door. Her sobs were quieter now, muffled as her damp face pressed Charlene's bare throat. Charlene rubbed her hand soothingly over the small back.

Earlier that day, Melissa had helped Charlene move a changing table and rocking chair into the empty bedroom next to the triplets' room. The babies still refused to fall asleep unless they were all in the same room—they fretted and worked themselves into a state if the adults tried to separate them. Nevertheless, Charlene was determined to find a solution to their waking each other in the night. If one of them cried, the other two inevitably woke, and the loss of sleep for everyone was a problem that desperately needed solving.

Charlene managed to ease Jessie back, putting an inch or so between them, just enough to unzip her footed pajamas. The pink cotton was damp, as was the diaper beneath.

"Let's change your clothes before we get your medicine," she said, lowering Jessie to the changing table.

The little girl whimpered in complaint and when Charlene stripped off the damp pajamas, Jessie's little mouth opened and she wailed.

In the bedroom next door, one of the other triplets protested and then began to sob. Charlene groaned aloud. The sound was bound to wake Nick.

She took Jessie's temperature with a digital ear thermometer, relieved when it registered only a degree above normal. As she quickly replaced Jessie's wet diaper with a dry one and tucked her into clean pajamas, Charlene fervently wished the employment agency would find a suitable nanny applicant soon. If the triplets had two nannies—herself and another—then maybe Nick wouldn't feel required to get up at night when the babies woke.

And she wouldn't be confronted with seeing him in the pajama bottoms he'd started sleeping in after that first night when he'd staggered into the triplets' bedroom in navy boxers. He might believe he'd found a modest alternative to underwear, but as far as she was concerned, the low-slung flannel pants only made him look sexier.

The low rumble of Nick's voice as he talked to the babies carried through the wall separating the rooms and Charlene was certain both Jackie and Jenny were awake.

"Come on, sweetie," she murmured to Jessie, lifting her.

She left the room and paused in the doorway of the triplets' bedroom. Nick had Jackie in one arm and Jenny in the other. Both babies were sobbing, blankets clutched in tiny fists.

"Jessie's temperature is up again. I'm taking her downstairs to get her medicine out of the fridge." Charlene had to raise her voice to make sure Nick could hear her over the crying babies. His brief nod told her he'd understood, and she headed downstairs, leaving him to cope with the two fractious little girls.

As she pulled open the refrigerator door and took out the prescription bottle, she heard Nick come down the stairs and go into the living room. Jackie and Jenny were still crying, although the volume wasn't quite as loud as before.

Jessie's sobbing had slowed to hiccups and intermittent outbursts. Charlene managed to unscrew the lid from the bottle and fill the eyedropper with the proper dose of pink medicine while balancing the little girl on her hip.

"Open up, sweetie." Fortunately, the medication was strawberry flavored and Jessie's mouth immediately formed an O. Just like a little bird, Charlene thought. Jessie's lips closed around the dispenser and Charlene emptied the pink liquid into her mouth. "Good girl, you like that don't…"

A sudden blast of music from the living room startled Charlene and she jumped, nearly dropping the bottle. Jessie's eyes grew round, her little body stiffening in Charlene's grasp.

"What in the world?"

The volume lowered as quickly as it had blared. The music didn't cease, though, and Charlene wondered why Nick felt a concert by Bob Seger was a good 1:00 a.m. choice for year-old babies.

Jessie, however, seemed to wholly approve of Nick's selection. She kicked her feet and gave Charlene a toothless grin.

"You like that?" Charlene replaced the lid on the bottle and returned it to the refrigerator. Then she took a baby wipe from the container next to the sink and smoothed the cool, damp towelette over tearstained downy cheeks, closed eyes and brow. When she wiped Jessie's mouth and chin, the little girl stuck out her tongue and left a faint pink streak across the baby wipe.

"Feel better?"

Jessie babbled a reply and Charlene nodded gravely. "Excellent. Let's go see how Uncle Nick is doing with your sisters. And let's ask him why he decided to have you all listen to rock 'n' roll before dawn."

She and Jessie reached the archway to the living room. Nick sat on the sofa, Jackie lying across his chest and Jenny sprawled on the soft leather cushion with her head on his thigh. Neither little girl was asleep but they'd stopped crying and appeared to be content. Rufus lay on the floor at Nick's feet, his head on his outstretched paws. He looked up at Charlene and wagged his tail, but didn't get up.

Charlene crossed the room and dropped into the

big armchair. Jessie laid her head on Charlene's shoulder, popped her thumb in her mouth, and was blissfully quiet.

"What did you do to them?" Charlene said, just loud enough to be heard over the music. Bob Seger had finished and she was fairly certain the current song was Tom Cochrane's "Life Is a Highway."

"They love music," Nick said simply. "I should have thought of this earlier."

"But this isn't exactly a lullaby," she said. "Great song, I love it. But not what a year-old baby usually likes."

"Not normal babies, maybe. But Stan and Amy loved music—all kinds of music. We never discussed it, but I'd be willing to bet the triplets have been listening to everything from Seger and Cochrane to Sinatra and Ella Fitzgerald since the day they were born. Probably before they were born," he added with a tired grin. Gently, he lifted Jenny and laid her facedown on her tummy on the sofa cushion beside him. She murmured, stirred, then went still.

"How did you figure it out?" Charlene lowered her voice to a whisper as the state-of-the-art sound system randomly selected tracks from CDs and segued smoothly from Cochrane to Ella Fitzgerald. The chanteuse's mellow tones, smooth as butter, alternately crooned and belted out the lyrics of "A Tisket, A Tasket."

"I remembered my mother telling me she used to sing us to sleep. When the girls woke up at the motel the other night, I sang to them—would have tried a lullaby but I didn't know one, and the only song that came to mind was a Bob Seger favorite." He shrugged and glanced down at Jackie, whose eyes were closed. One tiny fist clutched her blanket while the other held fast to a handful of the cotton pajamas covering his thigh. "I don't have the greatest voice, but it worked—so I thought I'd try the real thing."

"I think you've discovered the magic bullet," Charlene said, smiling at him. "They're sound asleep."

He smiled back, laugh lines crinkling at the corners of his eyes. His hair was rumpled from sleep, his jaw shadowed with beard stubble and his big body sprawled on the sofa with a baby asleep on each side of him. The warm light from the lamp on the end table illuminated half of his face, brushing the arch of his cheekbones and the line of nose and jaw with gold, and threw shadows across the other.

"Sugar," he drawled, his eyes twinkling, "it's a good thing something finally worked. Because after days of little to no sleep, if we were married and these were our kids, I'd seriously consider divorcing you and giving you custody—just so I could have eight hours of uninterrupted sleep."

Charlene burst out laughing.

Jessie stirred, her eyelids lifting. Charlene immediately muffled her laughter, smoothing her palm in circles over the baby's back, and she drifted asleep once more.

When Charlene looked up at Nick, he was watching her through half-closed eyes. Her heartbeat accelerated, her lungs seized as she stared at him. Then his features shifted, erasing whatever she thought she'd glimpsed on his face, and his big body shifted restlessly against the cushions. She could no longer read his expression—was no longer sure the moment had even happened, or if she'd imagined the sudden blaze of sexual awareness she'd felt between them.

"I think it's safe to take them back to their cribs," he said, stroking one big palm over Jackie's back. The little girl didn't stir.

"At least Jackie," Charlene agreed. She glanced down at Jessie, who seemed as deeply asleep as her sister. "And Jessie. What about Jenny?"

"She's out like a light." Nick gently picked up Jackie and stood. "If you'll keep an eye on Jenny, I'll take Jackie up and come back."

Charlene nodded and he headed for the stairs, Jackie cradled in his arms. She turned to watch him go just as Ella reached the end of her song. A heartbeat later, the opening lyrics of Prince's "Little Red Corvette" thumped from the speakers and filled the room.

"I've got to stop watching Nick walk away from me," she muttered to herself. *We have a professional relationship, employer-employee, and ogling the boss's very fine backside is probably taboo. Not to mention embarrassing should he turn around and catch me staring.*

Rufus's tail thumped against the wood floor. Charlene looked down at him and found him eyeing her, pink tongue lolling, ears alert.

She could swear he was laughing.

* * *

The following morning, Charlene wanted nothing more than to hit her alarm clock's Snooze button and roll over for another hour of sleep. But she knew if she didn't shower and have her coffee before the triplets awoke, she wasn't likely to do so until their afternoon nap.

She barely had time to pour a cup of coffee and say good-morning to Nick when he entered the kitchen to fill his travel mug before Melissa arrived. Nick left for the office moments later and the purr of the Porsche's engine had barely trailed away to silence outside when LouAnn knocked on the back door. The triplets awakened soon after, and the day's chaos began. When the babies napped after lunch, Charlene fell into bed and slept dreamlessly.

Just about the time that Charlene was catching her much-needed nap, Ross Fortune arrived in Nick's office for their meeting.

"Ross. Good to see you." Nick shoved his chair back and stood, leaning across the desk to shake his cousin's hand. He hadn't seen Ross since the New Year's Eve party at Red Restaurant. His brown hair was longer, brushing his shoulders. On a less rugged man it might have looked effeminate. On Ross, the long hair had the opposite effect. "Have a seat."

Ross sat in one of the two chrome-and-leather chairs facing Nick's desk and took a small notebook and pen from the inner pocket of his jacket. "I appreciate your cooperation in agreeing to see me today. I know it was short notice."

"No problem." Nick dropped back into his chair, leaning back and linking his fingers across his midriff. "I'm happy to do anything that might help you find out what's going on with the family."

"Good." Ross's brown eyes were shrewd, his gaze direct. "Give me the highlights."

Nick's eyes narrowed. "Someone slipped a note into Patrick's pocket at Red Restaurant during the New Year's party. He called us all together at the Double Crown last month to tell us about it."

"What did the note say?"

"'One of the Fortunes is not who you think,'" Nick quoted, shaking his head. "Makes no sense, at least as far as I can tell. We all thought it was the first contact in a blackmail attempt, but everyone at the meeting insisted they had no idea what it could mean, nor who the blackmailer might be."

"Hmm." Ross glanced at his notes, flipped a couple of pages, and looked back at Nick. "And there have been three more notes?"

Nick nodded. "My dad received one—so did Cindy. That's when your mom suggested we contact you and begin an official investigation." Nick saw Ross's eyes shutter, his face unreadable. He knew Ross and his mother had problems—in fact, as the eldest of Cindy's four children, Ross had pretty much taken over the role of caretaker for his younger siblings. It looked like there were issues between the two that went deeper than a mother-son disagreement. "All three of the original notes said exactly the same thing," he continued. He didn't know Ross well enough to comment or question him about what, if anything, his response to Nick's naming his mother meant. "But then Aunt Lily received a fourth that was more threatening."

"And what did it say?"

"'This one wasn't an accident either,'" Nick quoted, his voice deepening as anger rose. "She got that after the second fire—the one at the Double Crown."

"The first was the restaurant that burned down?"

"Yeah." Nick said grimly. "Darr's fiancée, Bethany, could have easily died in the restaurant fire. And Darr could have died when the barn burned at the Double Crown." He leaned forward, his forearms resting on his desk, and pinned Ross with a level stare. "Whoever the hell is doing this has to be stopped before someone gets hurt."

Ross nodded, his keen gaze fixed on Nick. "There haven't been any other accidents or threats to anyone in the family?"

"Not that I'm aware of," Nick confirmed.

Ross tapped his pen against his notebook, a faint frown veeing his brows downward. "And no one in the family has any idea who might have sent the notes?"

"None."

"Are you aware of any skeletons that might be rattling in someone's closet? Any gossip about a family member having an affair? Anybody gambling? Anyone with a drug or alcohol habit?"

"No." Nick shook his head. "But I've lived in Red Rock for less than two months. Before that I was in L.A. and off the grid on up-to-date family gossip—you might want to ask Aunt Lily. She seems to have her finger on the pulse of what's happening with the Fortunes."

Ross nodded and jotted a note on his pad. "What about the Foundation?" he asked when he finished and looked up at Nick. "Any controversial deals or activity?"

"Not that I know of, although I've only been working here for about six weeks, give or take."

"I understand the Red Restaurant is owned by the Mendozas, and they have a long-standing connection to the Fortunes. Do you have any reason to believe the notes and the fire at the Double Crown might be connected in some way to the Mendozas rather than the Fortunes?"

Nick shook his head. "I'm the wrong person to ask, I'm afraid. My dad might have better information, or Uncle Patrick, or the Mendozas themselves."

Ross nodded and made another note. "I'll be honest with you," he said when he looked back at Nick. "It's time to call in the cops. This has gone beyond possible blackmail. Lives have been endangered and that last note seems to threaten the family with more arson fires."

"I agree," Nick said, nodding abruptly. "But Aunt Lily is dead set against calling in the police. She's adamant about keeping this inside the family."

"The cops can spread a wider net, use forensics on the notes…" Ross stopped, glancing down at his pad before continuing. "If the fire department is investigating the two fires for possible arson, they'll eventually turn their report over to the police."

"I sure as hell hope so," Nick said with feeling. "Nobody in the family wants to upset Lily. It would be good news if the fire chief suspected arson and the department investigators could tie the two fires together, then refer both cases to the police."

"In the meantime, I'll keep digging." Ross stood and so did Nick. "Thanks for your cooperation, Nick."

Nick shook Ross's outstretched hand and walked him to the door. "Anything I can do to help, just ask. I know Darr feels the same."

"Good. I need to talk to him too." Ross took a business card from his pocket. "Would you ask him to give me a call? On my cell phone, not my office number."

"Be glad to."

After Ross disappeared down the hall, Nick placed a call to Darr but got his answering machine. After leaving a brief message to phone him, Nick hung up and walked down the hall to the coffee machine before returning to his desk and the cost analysis file he'd been working on earlier.

It occurred to him that he had more than the Fortunes to worry about now. Charlene and the triplets were living in his house, under his protection.

The possibility that their proximity to him and the rest of the Fortunes might have placed them in danger sent a surge of fierce anger through him.

Ross better solve this mystery—and fast.

But why didn't Lily want the cops brought in? Not

for the first time, Nick wondered if she was trying
to protect someone.

Could she be afraid of what the police might
uncover?

Much as he cared for Lily, he thought grimly,
Charlene and the babies had to be protected. If
Ross didn't find answers, and soon, he'd go to the
cops himself.

Chapter Five

Later that evening, with dinner over and the little girls tucked into their cribs for the night, Charlene made a pot of decaf coffee and carried a tray with the carafe, two mugs and a plate of Melissa's chocolate-chip cookies into the living room. She set the tray on the coffee table just as Nick's boots sounded on the stairs.

"Here's the first box," he said as he entered the room and dropped the carton on the floor in front of the sofa.

"The *first* one?" Charlene said dubiously, eyeing the box. She wasn't great at estimating size, but the cardboard box looked at least twelve inches deep and two feet square.

"There's another one just like it upstairs." Nick glanced at her, half-smiled and shrugged. "You don't have to do this, Charlene. Much as I appreciate your help, it's going to be boring. I'm sure the official nanny job description doesn't include shuffling through the boss's old photographs."

"I'm sure it doesn't," Charlene said dryly. "But I promised to help and I will." She dropped onto the leather sofa cushion and took a stack of photos from the box.

"I brought down this picture of Stan's family," Nick said, handing her a five-by-eleven photo. A wedding party was frozen in time, smiling and happy. "This is Lana."

He tapped the photo with his forefinger.

Charlene studied the young bridesmaid's facial features, noting the dark hair and athletic build until she was sure she'd recognize the triplets' aunt. Then she gathered a handful of photos and began to skim them.

On the sofa beside her, Nick settled back with a lapful of pictures. He thumbed through a stack of snapshots, paused to squint more closely at one, then tossed them into the reject pile atop the coffee table. Pretty soon the stack teetered and began to slide, glossy photos slithering across the oak table.

"Damn." He grabbed the pile and stood. Rufus lifted his head from his paws and eyed him expectantly. "I'll get an empty box to hold these. Otherwise they'll be all over the floor."

The big dog padded after him as he left the room.

Charlene continued to sort through the jumbled photos on her lap until she reached a colored snapshot of three teenage boys taken on a beach. Behind them, the ocean was bright blue. A younger Nick had an arm slung around the shoulder of one of the other boys, a surfboard lying on the sand beside him. His hair was shaggy, much longer than his current spiky cut, and his lean body was bronzed, white surf shorts hanging low on his hips.

Charlene studied the picture, her lips curving in a smile.

I bet you broke hearts in high school.

Reluctantly, she shuffled the photo to the bottom of her stack and continued to search for Amy's sister. Several photos later, she stopped abruptly. In what was clearly a professional studio portrait, a baby smiled out of the simple frame. A thatch of black hair and dark eyes, combined with the wide grin were inescapably Nick's features.

She trailed her fingertips over the photo, tracing the curve of his smile. Nick had been a darling baby and she couldn't help but wonder what his own children would look like. Would they inherit his charming smile and thick-lashed dark eyes?

What if she and Nick had children—would they be born with her thick auburn mane or with his black hair? And which gene would dominate to create their eye color, his dark brown or her own green?

With a start, Charlene realized she needed to get a grip. *Nick Fortune isn't interested in having babies with you,* she told herself, determinedly slipping the baby photo to the back of the stack. She continued to methodically scan the pictures, searching for Amy's sister while consciously refusing to allow herself to linger over the snapshots of Nick.

By the time he returned and held out a nearly empty carton, she'd finished searching through her stack of pictures and gathered them up, dropping them into the box. With Nick's entries, they made a formidable pile.

"So, how did you happen to buy a house this big?" Charlene asked, desperate to get her mind off her fantasies. "It seems huge for only one person."

"It's a lot of space," Nick admitted, glancing around the big living room as he dropped onto the sofa once more and picked up another handful of photos. "But the previous owners had already bought another house in Dallas and were anxious to move, so I got a great deal. I needed a place to stay in Red Rock, didn't want to rent, and this is a good investment." He scanned the sparsely furnished room once again and frowned. "I keep thinking I should buy some more furniture. I guess I'll get around to it sooner or later, if I decide to stay in Red Rock."

Surprised, Charlene looked at him. "Are you thinking of moving?"

"At some point, probably, but I don't have any definite plans." He thumbed through a small sheaf of photos and tossed them into the reject carton. "I moved here from Los Angeles a month ago to spend time with my brother, Darr."

"But I thought the Fortunes had settled in Red Rock for generations. In fact, I thought the family was a local institution." Charlene tried to remember where she'd heard that, but couldn't recall if someone had told her when she'd first arrived, or if she'd assumed it because the Fortunes were often referred to as a prominent local family. As it turned out, the three years she'd lived in Red Rock meant she'd been a resident for much longer than Nick.

"Not my branch of the family. I was born in California—grew up in a beachhouse in Malibu. My brother, Darr, moved to Red Rock a while back—then he talked me into moving here to work at the Foundation." Nick gathered a handful of photos from the slowly diminishing pile in the storage box. "How about you? Were you born in Red Rock?"

She shook her head, her hair brushing her shoulders. "No, I lived in Amarillo all my life until college."

"What brought you here?"

"A job offer after I graduated." Charlene didn't want to tell him the move hadn't been her decision. She would have preferred to begin her postcollegiate life in Amarillo. Barry had been the one who chose to accept a job offer in Red Rock, and she'd reluctantly agreed when he'd asked her to move here too.

"When we met on the plane, were you moving back to Amarillo to be closer to your mother?" Nick said.

"Something like that," Charlene replied, not wanting to go into an explanation of her breakup with Barry. "But then she told me she'd met Lloyd and he'd moved in with her—I knew I needed a change of plans."

"And thank God you did." Nick eyed her across the width of leather sofa cushion that separated them.

"I'm sorry your original plan didn't work out, but if it had, you wouldn't be here. And I don't know what I'd do with the triplets without you."

Sincerity rang in his words and a warm glow of satisfaction filled Charlene. "Thanks, Nick. It's always nice to be appreciated."

"Are you planning to go back to Amarillo after I turn the triplets over to Lana and her husband?"

Nick's question wiped the smile from her face.

"I hadn't thought that far ahead. I suppose so." She realized she truly hadn't given a thought to what she'd do after the triplets no longer needed her. Once their aunt took custody, Nick would return to being a bachelor. He certainly wouldn't employ a nanny. She wouldn't have a reason to see him again.

She frowned at the photos in her hand. Why did the prospect of not seeing Nick on a regular basis bother her so much? She barely knew him. In fact... She mentally counted the days since they'd shared an airline flight. Was it really less than a week?

How could she have become so attached to Nick and the triplets in such a short time?

Granted, it had been an intensive few days, but still...

She looked sideways through her lashes at Nick. He was frowning down at a photo with fierce concentration.

"Did you find something?" she asked.

"Maybe." He leaned across the sofa toward her, his forefinger pointing out a woman in the snapshot.

"Amy sent this in a card at Thanksgiving last year. See the girl standing with Lana?"

Charlene bent over the picture, eyes narrowing as she focused. The tangle of jungle was a backdrop for several rough huts surrounding a white wooden building. A woman easily recognizable as Lana stood on the porch steps, her arm around a pregnant young native girl. They both smiled happily into the camera.

"Who is she?"

Nick flipped the photo over but there was only a date—November 15th—scribbled on the back. "Damn. Amy didn't write details." He turned the photo faceup. "I remember talking to Stan and Amy around Thanksgiving, though. Lana had called from Africa and told them she and her husband were thinking of leaving their jobs to take over a privately owned center. Lana wanted to establish a clinic for women and provide prenatal care. Amy asked me if I'd volunteer accounting and financial services for the clinic if Lana could make arrangements with the local government to back the plan. This photo was taken at the center—Amy wanted me to see an example of how young the mothers are that Lana would be helping." He frowned and ran his hand over his hair, rumpling it, as he tried to remember. "I never heard whether Lana and her husband went through with the plan, but since they've dropped out of sight, maybe they did."

"But why wouldn't they have told Amy and Stan where they were going?"

"Stan said Amy hoped her sister wouldn't follow through with the idea because the center was in an isolated area. Maybe there isn't Internet service there—or phones." He looked grim. "Or maybe something happened to them."

"Don't even think it." Charlene fervently hoped nothing had happened to Lana and her husband. The possibility that the triplets might have lost their only remaining blood relative was too awful to even consider. "Is there anything in the photo that might tell you where the private clinic is located?"

They both bent over the snapshot.

"The sign above the porch overhang…I can't read it, can you?" Charlene asked, trying to decipher the faded lettering painted on the rough siding.

"Only a couple of letters. Not enough to know what the word is." Nick studied the photo intently before he gave up. "I'll take it to the office with me tomorrow and ask a friend in the Foundation's publicity department to take a look at it. He has a computer program that scans and enlarges without losing detail. Maybe he can identify the rest of the letters."

"And maybe that will give you the name of the place Lana and her husband have relocated to." Charlene mentally crossed her fingers that the results would be good.

"With any luck, they're one and the same. Although there's no way of knowing until the investigator checks it out." Nick glanced at his watch before he stood, tucking the photo into his shirt pocket. "It's getting late, we'd better call it a night.

At least it's Saturday tomorrow and I don't have to go to work. Although," he added dryly, "I doubt the triplets understand the concept of sleeping in on the weekend."

Charlene rose too, dropping the handful of photos she hadn't yet looked at into the first box. "Do you want to go through the rest of these?" she asked, waving at the box, its pile of photos much smaller. "Or will you wait until the investigator gets back to you about the clinic photo?"

"Might as well keep looking," Nick replied as he stacked the boxes and carried them into the hall.

Charlene followed, snapping off the lamp as she went. Rufus padded after her, leaning his head against her thigh when she stopped at the foot of the stairs. She rubbed his ears and he closed his eyes with a low rumble, leaning more heavily against her.

The muted cry of a baby sounded from upstairs, the whimper carrying easily to the three in the hallway.

Rufus's ears lifted and he swung his head toward the stairway.

Charlene's fingers stilled on Rufus's silky fur and she froze, listening intently. Almost immediately on the heels of the outcry, Willie Nelson's gravelly voice rasped out the opening bars of "Pancho And Lefty."

When she didn't hear another sound from the triplets, Charlene looked across the foyer. Nick stood at the open hall closet door, just as frozen as she. The silence stretched, broken only by the lyrics from Willie. Nick's taut body relaxed. He winked at her and his mouth curved in a heart-stopping grin.

"Looks like it worked." He shut the closet door and strolled toward her.

"Wiring the sound system into the girls room was a brilliant idea. And making it sound-activated was even better. Do you think it will keep them asleep all night?" she asked.

"I have no idea." Nick shrugged. "But it's a good sign the system came on and the girls fell back to sleep just now." He yawned and scrubbed his hand down his face. "I sure as hell hope it works every time they wake up. I could use the sleep—and I'm sure you could too."

"Absolutely," Charlene said with heartfelt conviction.

Rufus nudged her hand, his tail wagging as he rumbled.

"He needs to go out," Nick said. "I'll take him." He snapped his fingers and Rufus left Charlene's side.

"See you in the morning," she called after him as Nick and the big dog headed toward the kitchen.

He looked over his shoulder at her, his eyes darker, unreadable. "Sleep well."

Charlene waited until they disappeared down the hall before she climbed the stairs.

I'm getting way too attached to that man.

Admitting it didn't make the knowledge any less palatable, she realized with annoyance.

The following morning, Nick and Charlene had the girls to themselves, since Melissa didn't work on weekends.

"Let's walk down to the coffee shop," Nick suggested as he lifted Jenny out of her high chair. Elbows stiff and arms straight, he dangled her in front of him while he walked to the sink.

Charlene automatically grabbed a baby wipe from the container on the counter and handed it to him. He set Jenny on the edge of the counter, holding her firmly with one hand while he applied the towelette to the oatmeal smeared over her cheeks and chin.

"I'm sure the girls would love it, but are you sure you're up for it?" Charlene asked, eyeing him dubiously.

"Sure, why not?" he replied, concentrating on washing sticky spots off Jenny's face as she wiggled and squirmed, protesting. Finally, he tossed the towelette in the trash, perched the now clean Jenny on his hip and looked at Charlene. "What? You don't think I can survive taking them on a twenty-minute walk?"

Clearly, he'd read her expression and knew she had reservations about his ability to endure an outing with the three babies. "Have you got earplugs and tranquilizer pills in your pocket?"

"Very funny," he said with amusement, the corners of his mouth curving upward. "You obviously have no faith in me. I survived the drive from Amarillo here to Red Rock, didn't I? I've won my stripes. I can handle a walk to the coffee shop."

Charlene rolled her eyes but couldn't stop the answering smile that tugged at her lips. "All right. But remember, this was your idea."

"We'll take Rufus too."

Charlene didn't comment. A half hour later, after a search for Jackie's blanket and a last-minute change of diaper for Jenny, they finally left the house.

"We're a parade," Nick commented.

He pushed the girls' stroller and Charlene walked beside him, holding Rufus's leash. The dog trotted beside the girls, his wagging tail whacking the stroller's sunshield with each stride. Seated closest to him, Jessie laughed and grabbed for Rufus's tail but missed. Tongue lolling, he veered closer and licked her face. She grimaced and chortled, pounding the stroller tray with delight.

"Rufus, stop that!" Charlene commanded.

"It's just a little dog spit," Nick told her. "It won't hurt her."

"That's such a guy thing to say," she said, frowning at him. "Who knows what he's been eating in the backyard this morning."

"Probably dirt from the rocks he chews on. A little dirt won't hurt Jessie. In fact," he looked sideways at her, "I read an article on the Internet the other day that said kids today are too clean. Too many parents use antibacterial soap to keep kids from catching germs and they don't develop antibodies when they're little. Makes them susceptible later in life."

Charlene was stunned. She didn't know which was more surprising, that Nick was reading child-rearing articles online, or that he thought the girls should eat dirt.

"So you're advocating adding dirt to the girls' diet?"

"No, but I am saying that being licked by Rufus isn't likely to harm Jessie. And she likes it." He pointed at the little girl, squealing with delight when the big dog trotted close enough to enable her to grab a fistful of fur.

Rufus veered away from the stroller, leaving a handful of hair in Jessie's closed fingers.

"Jessie, don't eat that!" Charlene reached down and pried strands of dog fur from the baby's fist just as Jessie was about to shove her hand into her open mouth.

Nick stopped pushing the stroller, waiting while Charlene bent over Jessie and brushed away the remaining strands of brown fur that clung to her fingers.

"Okay, so I can see why we wouldn't want her to eat dog fur," he conceded when Charlene eyed him with exasperation. "Think she'd get fur balls?"

Charlene burst out laughing.

"I think you're getting punch-drunk from lack of sleep," she told him. "I know I am."

"I noticed the girls don't seem to be bothered," he said as they resumed walking.

"That's because they catnap during the day. Probably building up their strength to keep us awake at night," Charlene added darkly. Even though she'd only gotten up once with Jessie, all of the girls had stirred several times during the night and set off the audio system. While she was thankful she hadn't had to go into their room more than once, being wakened by the music still broke her sleep.

"Did your siblings do this when you took care of them?" he asked.

"Sometimes, but certainly not every night, and not on a regular basis," she said. "Usually there was a reason—like they were teething, or they had a cold, or something. But the triplets seem to wake when nothing's wrong. Often, the one that cries first and wakes the others doesn't even have a wet diaper."

"Maybe all the changes they've gone through in the last two weeks have disturbed them to the point that they can't get back to a normal routine."

"Possibly." Charlene glanced sideways at Nick. She couldn't read his eyes, hidden behind aviator sunglasses, but his lips were set in a straight line with no hint of humor. His expression had lost its earlier amusement. "But if that's what's going on, they'll find their balance," she said with quiet reassurance. "Children are resilient."

Rufus chose that moment to bark loudly and bound forward, dragging Charlene with him. Startled, she held on, pulling on his leash in an effort to stop him. He out-muscled her, determined to reach a cat sitting on a lawn several yards ahead. Surprised, the cat leaped into defense mode and raced to a nearby tree, clawing its way up the trunk and out onto a limb before stopping to glare down at Rufus and Charlene.

"Look at the cat's tail," Nick said, grinning as he stopped the stroller on the sidewalk next to Charlene, Rufus and the tree with the cat.

The tabby seemed twice its former size, the fur all

over its body standing on end, including its tail, which looked like a bottle brush. It stuck straight up in the air and seemed to quiver with outrage. Rufus barked again, his ears alert with interest. The cat narrowed its eyes and spat, hissing in fury. "Rufus, I don't think the cat wants to play," Nick said dryly.

The big dog whined, paws dancing against the grass beneath the tree.

"Maybe the cat isn't feeling sociable, but Rufus clearly thinks he's found a friend," Charlene observed.

"Good thing the cat's up there and he's down here," Nick said. "Or Rufus might learn a lesson about unfriendly cats."

Rufus barked and the triplets pounded on the stroller tray, their excited shrieks adding to the noise.

Nick winced and grabbed Rufus's collar, towing him away from the tree while pushing the stroller ahead of them and several feet down the sidewalk.

Still holding the big dog's leash, Charlene gave one quick glance at the tree behind them, where the cat continued to hiss and glower.

"I'm not sure who's more disappointed that the cat wouldn't come down," she said with a laugh when the dog and the triplets had subsided into relative quiet, "Rufus or the girls."

"If sheer noise could tell us, I'd say it's a toss-up." Nick released Rufus's collar and the big Lab ambled along, apparently having given up on the cat.

"Rufus is loud," Charlene agreed. "But I think the

triplets outweigh him when it comes to the length of time they can sustain decibels at an earsplitting level."

"That's because there are three of them and they can pace themselves. Two can keep yelling while the third one breathes," Nick argued. "Rufus has to stop barking to drag in air, and he doesn't have a backup buddy to keep the sound going."

"Who knew chaos could have such a logical analysis?" Charlene said, amused.

"I'm an analyst. It's what I do."

"And you apply the basics of your work to humans? And dogs," she added belatedly when Rufus tugged on her leash.

"Sometimes," Nick acknowledged.

She couldn't see his eyes behind the sunglasses, but she knew there were laugh lines crinkling at the corners.

When they reached the corner coffee shop, Nick tied Rufus's leash to a metal ring set into the wall. Charlene dropped into a chair at one of the little bistro tables, facing the triplets in their stroller.

"Are you okay here?" Nick asked, adjusting the sunshade atop the stroller seat to shade the triplets.

"Absolutely," Charlene replied, laughing at Jessie as she tried unsuccessfully to grab a handful of Rufus's tail.

"What do you want with your coffee?" he asked, grinning as Rufus managed to lick Jackie's face.

"Surprise me." Charlene eased the stroller out of the big dog's reach. Nick disappeared into the shop just as both dog and babies grumbled their disapproval of their forced separation. "Here, you three, have some water."

She handed each little girl a small sippy cup and they went silent, each sucking industriously on the opening in the lids.

"This is a healthy habit to develop, girls," Charlene told them. "Drink lots of water—it's good for you. And don't forget to eat lots of fruits and vegetables."

Three pairs of bright blue eyes watched her, apparently entranced, totally absorbed in what she was saying.

This is the thing about babies, she thought as she smiled at them. *They're fascinated by adults. They pay attention. Too bad they outgrow it later on.*

A small blue sports car zipped past on the street, slowing to wedge into a parking space halfway down the block. A couple got out, doors slamming, and walked toward Charlene.

The sun was at their backs, making it difficult for her to see them clearly, but there was something very familiar about the man. He walked with his arm slung over the woman's shoulders as they strolled nearer, apparently absorbed in each other and their conversation.

It wasn't until they drew nearer that Charlene realized the man was Barry.

Too late to run—and nowhere to hide. She knew precisely the moment when Barry recognized her, because he stopped abruptly, his jaw dropping in surprise.

"Charlene?"

"Hello, Barry," she said coolly, laying a restraining hand on Rufus's collar as he rose to his feet. A low growl rumbled in the dog's throat, his stance protective. "It's all right, Rufus," she soothed.

Barry looked from the dog to the three little girls in the stroller, and then back at Charlene, clearly puzzled.

"I thought you were in Amarillo."

"I was—for a day."

"And now you're back in Red Rock?"

"Obviously."

"With a dog and three kids?" The disbelief coloring his tones was palpable.

Since confirmation seemed unnecessary, Charlene looked at his companion and smiled. "Good morning."

The blonde eyed Charlene with a distinctly antagonistic narrowing of her eyes before she looked back at Barry. He was still staring as if dumfounded at the girls in their stroller. "Good morning," the blonde said finally, her tone cool but polite.

"Where did you get the kids?" Barry demanded.

"In Amarillo."

He glared at her, clearly annoyed by the brevity of her response.

She smiled back at him but didn't elaborate.

"I think I deserve an explanation." His voice held controlled impatience.

"Really?" she said coolly, lifting an eyebrow consideringly. "I can't imagine why."

Barry's face turned a deeper shade of red. Before

he could say anything further, the door to the coffee shop opened and Nick stepped out.

He set down two takeout cups of coffee and a bag on the tabletop. His eyes were still hidden behind the designer shades, but she knew with certainty that he'd swiftly assessed the situation. The two men couldn't have provided a stronger contrast—Nick with his dark hair and eyes, black T-shirt stretched across broad shoulders and chest, faded jeans outlining the powerful muscles of thighs and long legs. Barry's more slender frame seemed almost effeminate compared to Nick's well-toned body, while his blond hair seemed washed out in the bright sunshine, his skin pale next to Nick's California-sun-tanned features.

"I hope you like chocolate doughnuts," Nick said, shifting so he stood on her left and slightly in front of her, effectively placing himself between her and Barry.

The move was subtle but Barry clearly got the message. His face turned even ruddier and he fairly bristled at Nick.

"Who are you?" he demanded.

"Nick Fortune," he said with easy confidence, smiling at the woman with Barry.

Charlene had no trouble understanding why the blonde nearly melted into her hot-pink flip-flops.

"Hello," the woman breathed, clearly dazzled. "I'm Gwen."

"Pleased to meet you, Gwen." Nick smiled at her again and she batted her eyelashes, her smile widening.

Barry stiffened. The blonde met his angry stare

with cool aplomb before she looked back at Nick, ran her fingers through her hair and swept it back over her shoulders.

Well, well, Charlene thought. Instantly annoyed at the flirtatious gesture, she glanced at Nick. She couldn't see his eyes behind the sunglasses, but he seemed to have missed the blonde's invitation. He was turned toward Barry and his big body seemed to radiate menace.

Barry looked at Nick, his frown deepening.

"Fortune?" he said, unable to hide his disbelief. "Not one of the Fortune Foundation family?"

"Guilty, I'm afraid," Nick said.

Gwen seemed to suddenly become aware of the tension in the air. She glanced uneasily at Charlene. Charlene shrugged to indicate she was staying out of what appeared to be a brewing storm.

The blonde frowned and clasped her hands around Barry's arm, just above the elbow. "I'm dying for an ice cream, Barry." Gwen tugged determinedly. "Let's go in."

"I don't..." Barry began, resisting her urging as if he wanted to say more.

The triplets had been surprisingly quiet during the exchange. Jessie chose that moment to bang her sippy cup on the stroller tray, interrupting Barry as she babbled imperiously. Charlene turned to the girls, and out of the corner of her eye saw Gwen draw Barry away. A moment later, she heard the bell on the shop door jingle.

"Well, that was interesting." Nick dropped into the

chair next to her and took the lid off one of the cups. He slid the other coffee across the small tabletop to her and opened the bag. He took out a doughnut and bit into it, waiting until Charlene finished calming Jenny and turned back to pick up her cup before he continued. "So, who was he?"

"My ex-fiancé," she said calmly.

He paused, the doughnut halfway to his mouth, and stared at her. "You're kidding."

"No, I'm not." She frowned at him. "Why would you think I'm kidding about having an ex-fiancé? Do you find it impossible to believe that someone would want to marry me?"

"Hell, no." He frowned back at her. "I'm just surprised you said yes—he looks like a jerk."

"He's not," she denied. Then she considered her response and shrugged. "Okay, maybe he *is* kind of a jerk."

She had the distinct impression that Nick was rolling his eyes behind his sunglasses.

"No kidding." He finished his doughnut in one bite. "How long were you engaged?"

"We weren't actually officially engaged. He never gave me a ring. But we were together for three years."

"Three years, huh?" He took a drink of coffee and studied her over the cup rim. "Where did you two meet?"

"In college." She picked a doughnut from the bag and broke off a bite, popping it into her mouth.

"Let me guess—I bet he was in a drama class with you. Or was it a poetry class?"

She narrowed her eyes at him consideringly. "It was poetry. How did you know that's where we met?"

"Just a wild guess. He looks like the kind of guy who'd pick up girls in poetry class."

"He does?" Charlene considered Barry's blond hair, classically handsome features, a frame that might be called lanky but never muscled, and narrow, scholarly hands, without a callus to be found on the smooth, soft skin. "Hmm, I think I see what you mean."

"You said he was your *ex*-fiancé. What happened?"

"I suppose you could say we drifted apart in the years since college and grew to have different goals for our lives," Charlene said slowly, thinking about his question. The breakup with Barry had been coming for months. Their final argument had followed weeks of escalating bickering over a variety of issues, including whether they should pool their money and buy a house. It had ended with her walking out, their relationship over.

She could hardly believe only a few weeks had passed since they'd officially parted ways. So much had been packed into the last week with Nick and the triplets that it seemed much longer.

She'd dreaded running into Barry. She'd been sure it would be an awkward, emotionally painful encounter. But in fact, she realized, she'd felt very little beyond mild regret and annoyance.

What did that say about the depth of their attachment? Had she really loved him—or had they drifted into a relationship through sheer convenience and habit?

"When did you break up?"

"A few weeks ago."

"So that's why you were leaving Red Rock and flying to Amarillo?"

Charlene nodded. "I was going to stay with my mother while I found a new job and an apartment."

She rubbed her temples with her fingertips, feeling a headache coming on.

"You okay?" Nick asked.

His words interrupted her reverie, yanking her back to the present. She immediately ceased rubbing her temples and picked up her coffee.

"Of course. I'm fine. What was I saying?" She paused to sip her coffee, gaining a moment to recall his earlier question. "Oh, yes—being engaged. Actually, becoming un-engaged." She shrugged. "It's not uncommon for couples to discover they're not well-suited during a long engagement."

"If you say so." Nick looked at her over the rims of his sunglasses, his eyes intent. "Three years is a long time to be engaged."

"We wanted to establish our careers, save money for a house and so on."

"Couldn't you have done that after you were married?" His deep voice held a touch of derision.

"I suppose so, but it seemed wiser to wait until we were more settled." She frowned at him. "I suppose you would have leaped straight into marriage?"

"Damned straight," he said with emphasis. "If I

cared enough about a woman to ask her to marry me, I wouldn't be willing to put off the wedding for three years."

"And if *she* wanted to wait, I'm suppose you'd toss her over your shoulder and haul her off to your cave?"

His mouth quirked and he laughed. "No, I'm not that much of a caveman—although I'd be tempted." He stared at her for a moment. "Charlene," he said bluntly, "your ex-fiancé is a fool. He should have hustled you off to the altar the day you said yes. I'd never make that mistake."

Charlene felt her eyes widen. Her heart threatened to pound its way out of her rib cage. There was something about the intensity of his stare beneath lowered eyelids and the curve of his mouth that was more sensual than amused.

"I don't…" she began. She had to pause and clear her throat, her voice husky with the effort to speak. She lost track of what she'd been going to say when his gaze shifted from her eyes to focus on her mouth, lingering there for a long moment.

His lashes lifted and his gaze met hers. Charlene caught her breath. Focused male desire blazed in his eyes. She felt caught, unable to look away.

Behind him, the door to the coffee shop burst open and a crowd of teenagers poured out onto the sidewalk. Their laughter and raised voices was boisterous and loud, but it wasn't enough to break the web that Charlene felt spun out between her and Nick.

But then one of the boys bumped the back of Nick's

chair and he looked away from her, over his shoulder at the kid.

"Sorry." The teenager raised his hands in apology. "Didn't mean to do that."

"No problem." Nick's voice was clipped.

When he turned back, his face was blank and Charlene could no longer read his eyes.

"Ready to go?" he asked, rising to take his cup and the empty doughnut bag to the trash can.

"Yes, of course." Charlene followed suit.

Despite the distraction of the three babies and an energetic dog on the walk home, Charlene couldn't forget the heat in Nick's eyes. Nor could she ignore her reaction to the sexual tension that still sizzled in the air between them.

She pretended to be unaware, busying herself with Rufus's lead as they entered the house. The dog raced away, disappearing into the kitchen, and she turned to help Nick with the girls.

He bent to unhook Jessie just as Charlene moved. The resultant bumping of shoulders knocked her off balance, and Nick grabbed her, his big hands closing over her biceps to keep her from falling.

"Damn, I'm sorry—are you okay?"

"Yes…I, um…" She couldn't finish the sentence. He stood so close she could see the fine lines fanning at the corners of his eyes and the faint shadow of dark beard along his jawline. Bare inches separated their bodies, and his heat, combined with the subtle scent of aftershave and soap, urged her to close the distance and wrap her arms around him. The need to feel him pressed against her, breast to thigh, was overpowering.

His gaze searched hers, his frown of concern replaced with sensual awareness. His eyes narrowed; his hands tightened on her shoulders and he lowered his head. She waited, breathless, unable to tear her gaze from his.

Rufus bounded back into the room, barking as the babies greeted him with shrieks of delight.

For one brief moment, the two adults remained frozen.

Charlene thought she caught a flicker of frustration in Nick's eyes before he stepped back, releasing her.

"Rufus, down." His voice was deeper, gravelly.

She bent to unlatch Jessie from the stroller.

"Time for the girls' morning snack." Charlene knew she was blatantly using the babies as an excuse, but she needed to put space between herself and Nick.

If this morning was any example of how successfully she could handle her attraction to Nick, she was in big trouble.

Chapter Six

The following day was Sunday and the hours flew by. Caring for the triplets left little time for more personal discussions. Charlene was relieved when Nick seemed more than willing to keep conversation in neutral territory and far away from any deeply personal or potentially intimate subjects.

After Nick left for the office on Monday, Charlene felt tension drain out of her body like air from a punctured balloon. She had an entire day ahead of her to shore up her defenses and come to terms with the desire she'd read in Nick's eyes on Saturday. She wasn't sure it would be long enough.

Not that she hadn't been *trying* to do so every hour

since it happened. She just wasn't having a lot of success.

Improbable as it seemed, Nick was attracted to her.

She couldn't mistake or deny what she'd seen in his eyes. What she didn't know was whether he'd feel the same for any female he'd been thrown into daily contact with. Their situation—sharing a house, sharing the care of the triplets—was tailor-made to promote intimacy.

As she and Melissa cared for the triplets, Charlene pondered the question. By noon, she'd decided that Nick was only reacting as any male would in their situation.

It's not me, she decided. Living in each other's pockets for a week had created a false attraction. Probably like survivors of a shipwreck who are stuck in the same lifeboat together.

Unwelcome though it was, she had to conclude that if she wanted to keep her heart intact, she had to ignore any shivers of longing she might feel for Nick.

The triplets were tucked into their high chairs in the big kitchen while she and Melissa monitored them as they tried to eat lunch. They missed their mouths more often than not, and it was a toss-up as to whether there was more food on the girls' faces, hair and clothes than in their stomachs. The women laughed as much as Jessie and Jenny when Jackie bent over and slurped applesauce directly from her bowl.

When she lifted her head, her mouth, chin, cheeks and the tip of her nose were covered with applesauce.

Jessie and Jenny shrieked and instantly copied Jackie, making smacking noises.

Charlene rolled her eyes and collected the dispenser of wipes from next to the sink and carried them back to the counter, holding the box out for Melissa to extract several before she removed three herself and set the box down within reach.

The phone rang as she and Melissa were removing sticky applesauce and peas from the squirming little girls.

"I'll get that." Melissa tossed stained towelettes in the trash and lifted the phone to her ear. "Fortune residence." She paused, listening. "Yes, she is, just a moment." She handed the phone to Charlene. "It's for you."

Surprised, she mouthed, "Who is it?" but Melissa only shrugged.

"Hello?"

"Charlene? This is Kate."

Hearing her friend and former coworker's voice instantly had Charlene smiling with surprise and delight. The swift exchange of hellos and how are yous made her realize how insulated she'd been over the last week. She hadn't even taken time to let Kate know she was back in town.

"How did you know I was here?" she asked, curious.

"I called your mom and she gave me this number. Meet me for coffee," Kate demanded. "You've got to tell me why you're in Red Rock!"

"I can't—I'm working." She listened as Kate protested. Melissa looked up from wiping Jackie's fingers and lifted an inquiring brow. "No, really, I can't."

"If you want to go out, I can handle things here after the girls go down for their nap," Melissa said.

"Hold on a second, Kate." Charlene covered the mouthpiece with one hand. "Are you sure, Melissa?"

"Absolutely," the housekeeper said firmly. "You haven't been away from the babies since you got here. You should get out of the house. Go meet your friend."

"All right." She confirmed a time with Kate and rang off. "Thanks so much, Melissa. Kate and I used to work together. It'll be so nice to chat and catch up."

"No problem," Melissa assured her.

An hour later, Charlene and Kate sat at a table in the back of the neighborhood coffee shop. The café was nearly empty, the lunch rush over.

"I can't believe you didn't call me. When did you come back to Red Rock?" Kate asked.

"About a week ago, maybe a bit more. Days and nights are just a blur. I've been seriously sleep deprived up until a couple of days ago and I haven't caught up yet."

Kate's dark brows zoomed upward. "Why? What are you doing—or shouldn't I ask?"

"I'm working as a nanny."

Kate stared at her blankly. "A nanny? You left a perfectly good job at the hospital to babysit?"

Charlene chuckled and sipped her iced tea. "Hearing you put it in those terms, it does sound pretty illogical, doesn't it?"

"You think?" Kate rolled her eyes. "Why did you do it?"

Charlene spent the next few moments reciting the sequence of events leading to her accepting Nick's job offer. When she was done, Kate was speechless.

"So, here I am." Charlene waved her hand, indicating the café's interior and the greater world of Red Rock beyond the glass windows. "Back in Red Rock. And working as a nanny."

"I'm not sure where to start," Kate told her. "I've got a dozen questions. Let's get right to the big item on my list." She glanced around the sparsely populated café then leaned forward, elbows on the table, and whispered. "Is Nicholas Fortune as drop-dead gorgeous as rumor says he is?"

Charlene almost choked on her coffee. She leaned toward her friend and whispered back, "Yes. Definitely."

"Ah." Kate's dark eyes twinkled. "I knew there was more to this story than your needing to find a job superquick."

Charlene told her about the bonus offer, grinning as her friend's eyes widened and she gasped.

"Geez, why didn't I meet him first?" Kate groaned. "I'd work as a nanny for that kind of money. That's amazing."

"That's what I thought. I couldn't afford *not* to take the job. And given how desperate I was to get out of my mom and Lloyd's way, the bonus was just icing on an already great cake."

"What are you going to do with all that money—stash it in a 401K?"

"Part of it, probably. I might go back to school for my master's."

"Great idea," Kate said, nodding with enthusiasm. "So nice to have options. Have I mentioned that I'm green with envy?" She added. "Daily contact with the gorgeous Nick Fortune, *and* you're making incredible money for this gig. Life surely couldn't get any better."

Unless Nick is interested in me for more than my babysitting skills. Charlene didn't voice the thought aloud. She didn't want anyone, even Kate, speculating about her feelings for Nick. She didn't doubt they'd remain unspoken by her and unacknowledged by him.

"We should celebrate," Kate went on, obviously unaware of Charlene's lack of comment.

"We are celebrating." Charlene lifted her tea and saluted her friend.

"No, no—we need to celebrate with champagne and a night on the town."

"I'd love to—but I don't have any nights off."

"What? That's not right."

"I'm the triplets' primary caretaker during evenings and overnight. I can take a little time off during the day when Melissa is at the house, but not at night."

"That's got to be illegal. Aren't employers required to give an employee set times for coffee breaks, lunch, dinner, et cetera?"

"I'm sure they do, but this isn't a normal work situation. In fact, the job is only temporary. Once the girls' aunt is found and she arrives to take custody of them, my job will be finished. And I don't mind working long hours."

As she said the words, Charlene realized that when Lana arrived to collect the triplets, she would have to say goodbye—to both the girls and to Nick.

And no amount of bonus money was going to make it easier to walk away.

At the very moment Charlene was joining Kate for coffee at the café, Nick's cell phone rang across town just as he returned to his office after lunch. A quick glance at Caller ID had him grinning.

"Hey, J.R., what's up?" Nick greeted his older brother enthusiastically. The rest of the world might use his given name of William, but to his close friends and family he was always J.R.

"Not much. How's it going in Texasville? Are you wearing a ten-gallon hat yet?"

Nick laughed at his older brother's teasing. "I told you when I left L.A.—I don't think I'm the John Wayne type."

"Too bad," J. R. Fortune drawled. "Women love cowboys."

"Yeah," Nick said wryly. "So I've heard."

"How's the new job?"

"I'm still settling in, but it's going well."

"And what about life in a small town? How's that working for you?"

"A few challenges, but that only makes life more interesting, right?" Nick said, carefully noncommittal.

"What kind of challenges?" J.R.'s tone told Nick

that his attempt at evading his brother's question hadn't worked. J.R. knew him too well.

"Hasn't Darr told you?"

"I haven't talked to Darr. He called and left a message—I returned the call and got his machine. We keep missing each other."

"Then you haven't heard I've become a father."

The statement was met with dead silence.

"Uh, you want to explain that?" J.R. said finally, his voice carefully neutral.

"I'm the guardian of three baby girls—one-year-old triplets."

J.R.'s swift, drawn-out expletive was a testament to his shock. It wasn't often J.R. was caught off guard.

"First of all, they're not mine," Nick said, taking pity on his brother. "Not by blood, anyway—they're Stan and Amy's little girls. I have temporary custody until the estate's attorney locates Amy's sister, then she'll take them."

"Damn."

For the next few moments, Nick and J.R. had a nearly word-for-word repeat of his conversation with Darr.

"You're the last person I'd expect someone to leave their kids to," J.R. said finally. "Especially little girls. And especially three of them at a time. How the hell are you taking care of them, anyway? I can't see you changing diapers. Did you hire staff?"

"My housekeeper went from part-time to full-time, and I hired a nanny."

Something in his voice must have given him away, because J.R. pounced on the comment.

"Yeah? What's she like?"

Irritated, Nick swung around in his chair and glared at the window in front of him. "That's the same question Darr asked me. She's female. She takes care of the kids. What else is there?"

"Yeah, right." J.R.'s drawl held a wealth of disbelief. "If there wasn't something else, you wouldn't care if I asked."

"She's female," Nick repeated. "She has red hair. She's around twenty-five, maybe twenty-six. And she's beautiful." He bit off the words.

"And she's living in your house?"

"Yeah, she lives in the house."

"Okay, okay. Don't be so touchy. Did I ask you if you were sleeping with her?"

"No," Nick growled. "But you were thinking it."

"Well, maybe," J.R. conceded, amusement coloring his tone. "But if our roles were reversed, you'd be wondering the same thing about me."

"I'm her boss," Nick said wearily. "She's a…very nice, very *young* woman."

"Well, that's good. If she's going to take care of your best friend's kids, then she needs to be an upstanding citizen. How does Rufus feel about her?"

"He's crazy about her." Nick half-grinned, remembering the goofy, adoring expression on the big Lab's face when Charlene rubbed his ears and said good-night. "The feeling seems to be mutual."

"She sounds like Mom."

His brother's voice held a deep note of affection. Nick considered the comment. "Yeah, she's a lot like Mom."

Molly Fortune had been a tomboy, and her easy-going, fun-loving nature made her a much-loved member of the sprawling Fortune family. Her death two years earlier had left her husband and sons grief-stricken.

"Then you'd better marry her," J.R. said.

"Marry her?" Nick sat upright. "I said she's beautiful. I didn't say I wanted to marry her. Where'd *that* come from?"

"Any woman that reminds you of Mom has to be serious marriage material."

"Yeah, but I'm not serious about marriage."

"Not in the past," J.R.'s voice held amusement. "That was before you met the beautiful red-haired nanny."

"Doesn't matter. Even if I was the type to consider marriage, Charlene is too young for me—and way too smart."

"I get the age difference thing, although I don't agree with it. But what do you mean, she's too smart?"

"I don't know. I haven't asked her how many college degrees she has, but it wouldn't matter. What she's got doesn't come with a degree."

"What are you talking about?"

"She's very intuitive—she knows a lot about people. I haven't seen anyone yet that doesn't love her at first sight, including my dog." *And that idiot ex-fiancé of hers,* Nick thought. Despite Barry's hostile attitude, Nick was sure he hadn't misread the possessive vibes from Charlene's ex-boyfriend.

"All the more reason to marry her."

"I'm not getting married. I'm not serious about the nanny. Besides," he continued, "I'm her boss. She's strictly off-limits as long as she's working for me." Nick refused to consider the possibility of keeping Charlene in his life permanently. But thinking about how much he wanted her only drove him crazy with frustration.

"Sounds to me like you're blowing smoke," J.R. said. "Who are you trying to convince? Me? Or you."

"Let's change the subject. What's new with you?"

"I'm actually planning a trip to Red Rock—not sure when, but fairly soon. I'm thinking of making a few changes in my life, and since you and Darr like Texas so much, I thought I'd check it out."

"Damn, that's great news. Have you told Darr?"

"No, I haven't been able to reach him, remember?"

"Well, keep trying. If I see him, I'll tell him to call you. It would be great to have you living here."

"No promises," J.R. said. "I'll let you know when I have a firm date to visit. I want to meet your nanny—see if she really *is* anything like Mom. If you're really not interested, maybe I will be."

Nick ground his teeth but let the comment pass. Arguing with J.R. would only convince him that Nick was serious about Charlene.

And I'm not. Not even close.

Some small portion of his brain whispered that he was suffering from serious denial, but Nick refused to listen.

With both Charlene and Nick determined to keep their relationship strictly platonic and each other at arm's length, the next few days went by uneventfully. They focused on the girls while they were awake and retreated to their own rooms when the babies napped or went to sleep in the evening. Since the triplets were now consistently sleeping through the night, there were no more middle-of-the-night encounters in the babies' room.

On Thursday morning, Charlene woke early. It was still dark outside her window, the eastern sky only faintly beginning to brighten with dawn. Unable to fall back to sleep, she tossed and turned for another half hour before throwing back the covers and rising to take a quick shower, dress and apply light makeup. Moving quietly into the hall, she eased open the door to the triplets' room and peeked inside to find the three sleeping soundly. Certain she had an hour or two of uninterrupted quiet before the girls woke and her day began in earnest, she tiptoed down the stairs and into the kitchen.

She halted abruptly just inside the doorway.

The rich smell of brewing coffee filled the room, lit only by the small light over the stove. Nick stood next to the coffeemaker, his hips leaning against the countertop, arms crossed over his bare chest. Faded Levis covered his long legs, his feet bare on the tile floor. The muscled width of his chest was smooth, with only a narrow strip of black hair that started at his belly button and arrowed downward, disappearing beneath the low-slung waistband of his jeans. His shoulders and biceps, chest and abs were California tanned, padded with toned muscles that shifted and flexed when he moved.

He looked up and saw her. His eyelids lowered, shielding his eyes behind the thick screen of black lashes and making it impossible for her to read his expression.

"Morning." His voice was rusty, gravelly with sleep. His dark hair was tousled and damp, as if he'd rubbed it dry with a towel after his morning shower, then ran his fingers through it before heading for the kitchen and caffeine.

"Good morning." Charlene forced her feet to move. She crossed to the island and turned on her laptop. "You're up early."

"I have a meeting in San Antonio this morning." He yawned, dragging his hand over his eyes. "Thought I'd get an early start." He nodded at the coffeemaker. "Coffee should be done soon."

"Great." Charlene walked to the counter and opened an upper cabinet. She took down two pottery mugs and paused, glancing over her shoulder at Nick. "Do you want your travel mug?"

"Sure."

The metal mug with the UCLA logo Nick carried to work each morning was on the top shelf. She stretched, going up on tiptoe, but the mug was just beyond her fingertips. "I need a ladder," she murmured, trying to stretch another half inch.

"Here, I'll get it."

Before Charlene could step back and out of his way, Nick was behind her, bracketing her between his body and the countertop when he reached above her.

She was surrounded by him. The scent of clean soap and the faint tang of his aftershave enveloped her while the warmth of his body narrowed the brief distance between them even more. He leaned forward slightly as he picked up the mug and his bare chest brushed her shoulderblades.

Her breath caught in a faint, audible gasp, and she froze, immobilized as she struggled to deal with an overload of emotions.

Nick heard the quick intake of breath, felt the swift, slight press of her shoulders against his chest as she inhaled. He fought the fierce urge to claim and possess, his muscles locking with the effort. But then her rigidly held body eased slightly against his and his control slipped a notch.

He set the mug down and planted his palms on the countertop, bracketing her between his arms. The faint scent of flowers teased his nostrils and he bent his head until his lips nearly touched her hair, closing his eyes as he breathed in the smell of shampoo and warm woman.

She turned, her shoulder brushing against his chest, faced him, her back to the counter. Her green eyes were dark with awareness when her gaze met his, the curve of her mouth vulnerable. A spray of small freckles dusted the bridge of her nose and the arch of her cheekbones, golden against her fair skin.

Nick clenched his fists against the counter, muscles bunching in his biceps as he fought to keep from touching her. A lock of hair slipped out of the narrow clip holding it away from her face. Tempted beyond reason, Nick lost his battle and gently brushed the strand away from her cheek, tucking it behind her ear.

Her skin was as soft and silky as the bright threads of hair. Lured by the warmth under his hand, he traced his fingertips over the tiny freckles on her cheekbones then followed the smooth curve of her jawline. Her pulse fluttered at the base of her throat and he tested the fast beat with the pad of his thumb, his fingers and palm cupping the curve where shoulder met throat.

His gaze flicked up, met hers. Her green eyes were nearly black, a faint flush heating her throat and coloring her cheeks. Her lips were fuller, slightly parted, her breathing quicker.

The moment spun out, tension thickening the air between them.

"Tell me to step away," he rasped, his voice rougher, deeper than normal.

"I can't," she murmured.

"Why?"

"I don't want to."

"We shouldn't do this." His thumb stroked slowly, compulsively over the fast pound of her pulse point.

She lifted her hands and laid them, palms down, on his chest. Her fingers flexed and he groaned, his fingers tightening reflexively on her shoulder. Her gaze fastened on his mouth and she slid her arms higher around his neck, going up on tiptoe, her body lying flush against his.

Nick lost the struggle. He bent his head, meeting her halfway as her lips sought his.

Determined not to lose control, he pressed his fists against the countertop, resisting the urge to wrap his arms around her and press her close.

Equally determined not to give in to the raging need to devour her mouth, he brushed her lips with his, refusing to deepen the contact when she opened her mouth under his and licked his lower lip.

"You taste like honey and mint," he muttered against her mouth, changing the angle to taste the corner of her mouth. Primal satisfaction seared through him when she gasped and pressed closer.

"Stop teasing and kiss me," she demanded, frustration in her voice. She cupped the back of his head in her palms and refused to let him move away as she crushed her lips against his with pent-up desire.

Nick lost the ability to reason. He wrapped his arms around her and pinned her between his body and the counter behind her. Their mouths fused in a heated exchange.

On some distant level, he knew he had to stop this—

stop *them*—before he lifted her onto the counter and slipped off her clothes. He reached for control, struggled to bring them back from the precipice, until at last their breathing slowed.

He took his mouth from hers, her lips clinging in protest, and rested his forehead against hers while his heartbeat continued to slam inside his chest and thunder in his ears. "You're killing me," he murmured.

She eased away from him, just far enough to look up and search his face. "What do you mean?"

"I've wanted this since I looked up and saw you walking down the plane aisle," he told her.

"Really?" Her face glowed. "Me too."

"Don't tell me that." He groaned when his body leaped in response. "I'm having enough trouble keeping my hands off you. And you're off-limits. You work for me. I don't kiss employees."

"Then maybe I should quit." The bemused smile she gave him held a hint of mischief.

"I wouldn't blame you if you did," he said grimly. "But for God's sake, don't. The girls need you."

Her smile disappeared. Her thick lashes lowered, screening her eyes.

"Of course," she said, her voice cooler, more distant. "For a moment I forgot the circumstances."

She eased back, separating their bodies and putting a bare inch of space between them.

Somehow, Nick felt as if she'd moved across the room.

"I think I'll take my coffee upstairs. I have a few things to do before the girls wake up."

He wanted to drag her back into his arms and kiss her until the cool remoteness dissolved under heat and she was once again pliant and eager. But he knew it was far better that she'd put distance between them. He'd reached the limits of his control. If he spent much longer with her in his arms, he doubted whether he could make himself let her go.

"Right." He shifted away from her, leaning his hips against the counter, arms crossed, while he waited for her to pour her coffee and leave the room.

She didn't look back, her murmured goodbye and "have a good day" spoken over her shoulder, her face half-turned from him.

Then she was gone and he was alone in the kitchen.

He couldn't be sorry he'd kissed her. But now that he knew what she felt like in his arms, what her mouth tasted like under his, he knew keeping their connection strictly employer-employee was going to be damned near impossible.

Frowning blackly, his temper on edge, he filled his coffee mug and headed upstairs to finish dressing before heading for San Antonio.

Once safely in her bedroom, Charlene slumped against the wood panels and closed her eyes to blank out the light.

Stupid. That was so stupid, Charlene.

She never should have given in to the need to discover what it would be like to kiss Nick.

And it was mortifying to admit he would have walked away if she hadn't turned to face him, hadn't been the one to wrap her arms around his neck and instigate that kiss.

She nearly groaned with embarrassment. He was her boss. He'd said he didn't kiss his employees.

And it's against every principle I believe in to have an affair with my boss, she told herself. *So why didn't I stop?*

She'd never been tempted to break her own rules before. What was it about Nick Fortune that blew all her good intentions to dust?

She pushed away from the door and crossed to the bathroom. Running cold water, she pressed a dampened washcloth to her still-flushed cheeks, lowering it after a moment to stare at herself in the mirror.

"Nick is off-limits," she said to her reflection. "From now on, act as if this morning's kiss never happened."

Just how she was going to do that, she had no idea.

She hoped she was a better actress than she suspected, otherwise, Nick would know with one look that she was playing the role of disinterested woman.

And nothing on earth could be further from the truth.

On Saturday evening, two days after their fateful encounter in the kitchen, Andrew Sanchez telephoned. Nick and Charlene were in the upstairs bathroom, taking turns bathing the triplets before tucking them into their pajamas.

Nick left Jackie and Jenny chortling, happily sitting naked atop their damp towels on the bathroom floor, and stepped into the hall just outside the bathroom, covering one ear with his palm as he talked.

When he hung up, Charlene knew by his solemn, faintly grim expression that something had happened. Despite her vow to keep their conversations to business issues only, concern compelled her into speech. "Is something wrong?"

"The attorney in Amarillo found Lana and her husband."

"Oh." Charlene stared at him, torn between relief and dread. "Are they all right?"

"Yes."

"Where were they?"

"At the privately run clinic. The investigator used the information we found in the photo, flew to Africa and tracked her down. She's been out of touch because a river flooded and cut off the clinic from contact with the outside world."

"Are they on their way home?"

"Yes."

"How long before they arrive?"

"Sanchez wasn't sure—probably a few days, maybe a week, at most."

Which meant their time with the triplets was growing short, Charlene realized. Her arms tightened unconsciously, protectively around Jessie's chubby little body.

"I'm going to miss them," she said, her voice husky with emotion.

"Yeah. Me too." Nick's eyes roiled with emotion.

Playing on the floor at his feet, Jackie grabbed a fistful of Nick's jeans just below the knee and pulled herself to her knees. Nick broke eye contact with Charlene and went down on his haunches next to her. Jenny immediately crawled toward him too, babbling imperiously.

"Hey, you two. What are you doing? Are you trying to stand up, Jackie?"

The gentle affection in his voice brought tears to Charlene's eyes. She turned away, Jessie perched on her hip, and leaned over to fiddle with the tub, twisting the release to let the water drain. By the time she turned back, she had her emotions under control once more.

"I'll get Jessie ready for bed. Would you like me to take Jackie or Jenny too?"

"No, I'll bring them." Nick slipped an arm around each baby and lifted them as he stood. The babies gurgled and shrieked as they rose.

"You're a brave man," Charlene said in an effort to lighten the moment. "Neither of them are wearing diapers."

"I like to live dangerously," he replied with a half grin.

Later, when the girls were tucked into bed, Nick and Charlene stood in the hall outside their room.

"I think I'll read for a while before I go to sleep," she murmured.

"Wait." Nick caught her arm as she turned away, stopping her.

The feel of his warm fingers and palm on the skin of her bare arm sent heat shivering through her veins, making her heart beat faster. But the moment she stopped and turned back, he released her.

"Yes?"

"I meant to talk to you about this earlier, but after I spoke with Sanchez, I forgot…." He paused, thrusting a hand through his hair. "I want to take the girls to a party celebrating the reopening of Red. The Mendozas are longtime friends, and most of my family will be there. And I'd like you to come with me."

Charlene's brain stopped functioning. Had Nick just asked her out on a date? Then she realized he'd said he wanted to take the girls. He needed her help.

"Of course," she replied. "When is it?" She calculated swiftly when he told her the date. The opening would be before Amy's sister arrived to take custody.

They said good-night and Charlene headed down the hall to her room. She wanted time to come to terms with the sadness she felt, knowing that her time with the triplets would soon end.

She suspected Nick would miss the babies as much as she would.

Charlene knew the dinner at Red Restaurant wasn't a real date. It was a family affair, a chance for Nick to introduce the triplets to his extended family and friends. Despite sternly lecturing herself that she was accompanying them as an employee only, the evening of the grand reopening found her standing in front of her open closet, torn between choosing a sexy black cocktail dress or a less glamorous gown.

"Oh, get over yourself," she muttered impatiently. She scanned the contents of the closet and took a dress from a hanger. The black-and-white print was less likely to show food stains if one of the triplets tossed dinner at her, and the modest, scooped neckline wouldn't expose too much skin if one of the girls tugged it lower.

She stepped into the dress and pulled it on, zipping the side before standing back to look in the mirror. The dress was comfortable, the fitted waist and full skirt with its just-above-the-knee hem pretty but less figure-revealing than the body-hugging, midthigh hem of her favorite little black dress.

But the one I'm wearing is far more practical for an evening spent with three one-year-olds, she told herself.

She consoled herself by choosing frivolous, black, strappy sandals with three-inch heels before she slipped black pearl studs into her earlobes. Experience told her to skip a necklace, since the triplets delighted in playing and tugging on her jewelry. Instead, she settled for the matching black-and-white pearl ring.

Then she caught up a black clutch evening bag, tucked a few essentials into it, and left the room.

She heard LouAnn's distinctive raspy voice, followed by Nick's quick laugh, and followed the sound to the living room, pausing on the threshold.

LouAnn sat on the ottoman, her skinny frame bent at the waist as she supported Jenny. The little girl was on her toes, wobbling back and forth with a delighted grin.

Jackie and Jessie sat on the carpet, watching Jenny with fascination. All three of the little girls were dressed in matching blue jumpers with white knit blouses beneath, the neat Peter Pan collars edged in blue embroidery. They wore cute little patent-leather Mary Jane shoes with lace trimmed, pristine white socks. Each of them had a white satin bow in their black hair. They looked adorable.

Charlene purposely saved the best part for last. Her gaze found Nick, standing next to the stereo system. He wore black slacks that she was sure must have been tailored for him, a black leather belt and a white dress shirt with the cuffs folded back to reveal the gold Rolex on his wrist.

He looked over his shoulder at LouAnn, smiling as he watched her encourage Jenny. Then he looked past her and saw Charlene. His smile disappeared. His gaze ran from her face to her toes, then back again and something hot flared in his dark eyes.

"There you are," LouAnn said, breaking the spell that held Charlene. "Don't you look nice." She beamed and stood, picking Jenny up.

Charlene forced her gaze away from Nick and smiled at LouAnn. "Thank you."

"And you're right on time," LouAnn continued, waving a hand in the direction of the mantle clock. "You all better scoot or you'll be late."

"She's right." Nick walked toward them, pausing to pick up Jackie and Jessie. "The car's out front." He stopped in front of Charlene. "If you'll take Jackie, I'll collect the girls' diaper bag from the kitchen."

"Of course. Come here, sweetie," Charlene murmured, holding out her arms.

"I'll meet you at the car," Nick said, his face reflecting no emotion beyond casual friendliness.

"I'll carry Jenny out and buckle her in," LouAnn

said, leading the way. "I would have been happy to babysit the girls for you and Nick tonight," she continued as they followed the sidewalk around the front of the house and reached the SUV, parked on the drive in front of the garage. "But Nick said he wanted his family to meet them."

"Mmm hmm," Charlene murmured.

"I must say, I'm impressed by our Nick," LouAnn chattered on as the two women tucked the girls in their car seats and fastened buckles. "He's really stepped up to the plate to take care of these three. Not many confirmed bachelors would have changed their whole life to accommodate babies at the drop of a hat."

Before Charlene could agree with her, Nick joined them. Moments later, the diaper bag was stored away, Jessie was buckled into her car seat, and the SUV was reversing out of the drive to the street.

LouAnn stood in the drive, waving good-bye as they pulled away.

She's right, Charlene thought as the house disappeared in the rearview mirror. *Nick really has reacted in an exceptional way. If I were in desperate need of help, he's the person I'd want on my side.*

And as a woman, he's the man I want in my bed.

The unbidden thought brought a flush of heat to her cheeks. She glanced sideways at Nick. Fortunately, he was looking at the street as he drove, otherwise she was sure he would have known she was picturing him naked.

Chapter Seven

Nick ushered the girls and Charlene into the courtyard of Red and her eyes widened in surprise. Holding Jessie in her arms, she turned in a slow half circle.

"They've restored it just as it was," she exclaimed with delight. The square patio was tucked into the center of the building, edged on all sides with the dark walls of the restaurant. A fountain dominated the middle of the area. Its trickling water splashed against blue-and-white Mexican tiles, greeting diners with soft music. Several fan trees dotted the space, their green ribs draped with strings of tiny white lights. Tables were scattered around the courtyard, the underside of their colored umbrellas sporting more of the small white lights. Before the fire, the courtyard had boasted masses of old bougainvillea; these new plants were smaller, younger, but still colorful with bursts of vivid fuchsia, purple and gold. "This has always been one of my favorite restaurants in Red Rock, and I was hoping the new version would have the same feel."

"They wanted to rebuild as close to the original restaurant as possible," Nick confirmed. "The basic structure is an accurate replica, but some of the furnishings were irreplaceable. A few of the antiques dated as far back as 1845, when President Polk welcomed Texas into the Union." He nodded at the fan trees. "The trees and bougainvillea will need a few years to reach the size of the originals."

"But they will—in time," Charlene said.

"Nicholas!"

Charlene and Nick both turned to find Maria Mendoza moving quickly toward them, her husband José following more slowly.

Nick's face eased into a broad grin.

"How's my best girl?" he teased, bending to kiss the older woman's cheek.

She laughed and shook her head at him, the silver streaks in her black hair gleaming when the strands shifted against her shoulders. "Always the charmer." She beamed at Jackie and Jenny. Perched on Nick's arms, they each clutched a handful of his shirt in a tiny fist as they eyed her with open curiosity. Her gaze moved to Charlene and she lifted an eyebrow, a gleam of speculation in her dark eyes. "And who is this, Nicholas?"

"Charlene London, I'd like you to meet Maria and José Mendoza, the owners of Red and our hosts for the evening."

The adults exchanged pleasantries before Maria nodded at the triplets. "And are these adorable little girls your daughters, Charlene?"

"They're mine." Nick laughed when Maria's eyes widened with surprise. "Temporarily. I'm caring for them until their aunt arrives. Charlene took pity on me and agreed to help."

"They're beautiful," Maria enthused. "Aren't they, José?"

"Yes," the older man agreed, exchanging a very male look with Nick. Over six feet, José towered over his diminutive wife.

"What about your girls? Are they here?" Nick asked, glancing over the crowd.

"All three of our daughters and their husbands are here. Plus Jorge and Jane, of course—and even Roberto," Maria added with a proud smile.

Before Nick could comment, a waitress rushed up and whispered to José. He frowned and touched Maria's arm.

"I'm afraid we're needed in the kitchen—small emergency." He clapped Nick on the shoulder and smiled at Charlene. "Have fun, you two, enjoy your meal. I'm sure we'll see you later."

He ushered Maria away, following in the wake of the harried-looking waitress.

"I hope everything's okay," Charlene commented.

"I'm sure it's nothing José and Maria can't handle,"

Nick said. "Let's go inside and find a table—and some food."

They wound their way through the growing crowd on the patio, but it took them several moments to enter the restaurant. Nick seemed to know everyone present, and all of them wanted to say hello and ask about the triplets.

At last, they crossed the threshold and stepped inside the main dining room. Charlene was happy to see that here too, every effort had apparently been made to replicate the original ambiance and decor. Bright Southwestern blankets were displayed on the walls, together with paintings depicting battles between Mexican General Santa Anna and the Texans. A portrait of Sam Houston dominated one wall, next to a collection of period guns and a tattered flag in a glass case.

Guests sat or moved from table to table, visiting and eating beneath the glow of colorful lanterns hung from the ceiling.

"What a beautiful room," Charlene said. "Filled with beautiful people," she added with a smile.

Nick grinned back. "That's my family—the Fortunes are a handsome lot, aren't we?"

Charlene rolled her eyes. "And modest too."

He laughed out loud and shifted Jenny higher against his shoulder. "Yes, ma'am." He nodded toward an empty table just left of the center of the big room. "Let's grab a seat over there."

No sooner had Nick and Charlene settled the three girls into wooden high chairs and given their order to a waitress than Patrick Fortune and his wife Lacey stopped to say hello.

"It's a blessing you were available to help Nick with the babies, Charlene," Lacey said when introductions had been made all around. "We raised triplets too—three little boys. My goodness, what an experience that was!"

"Oh, yes." Patrick's eyes twinkled and he winked at Charlene. "I remember those days well—looking back, I'm amazed we survived it. Very little sleep, nonstop changing diapers and bottle-feeding—not to mention that the boys had an uncanny ability to synchronize catching colds and earaches." He shook his head. "Taking care of three babies is above and beyond the call of parenting duty."

"But they're worth every moment," his wife said fondly, slipping her arm through the crook of his elbow and laying her head on his shoulder.

"We realized that quite quickly," Charlene assured her. The two women exchanged a look filled with understanding. If all Nick's relatives were as genuinely likeable as the Mendozas and this couple, Charlene thought, she could easily understand why the Fortunes held such a powerful and respected position in the community of Red Rock.

Across the room, Maria Mendoza chatted with her cousin, Isabella, having left José to finish dealing with a minor menu mix-up in the kitchen.

"Nick seems very happy with his new family, doesn't he?" she said, smiling fondly at the gathering of Fortune family members at the table where the three little identical girls held court.

"Yes, he does," Isabella agreed, her gaze following Maria's. "I never would have imagined Nick being comfortable with children, but he's clearly enjoying them."

Just then, one of the little girls tugged the white satin bow from her hair and tossed it at Nick. It bounced off his sleeve and landed in his water glass. The adults at the table burst into laughter.

Maria and Isabella chuckled.

"They're darling little girls," Maria said. She sipped from her champagne glass and eyed Isabella over the rim. "I'm so glad you could be here tonight—I've been meaning to get in touch with you. I'd love to have you sell some of your blankets and tapestries at my knitting shop."

Isabella's eyes widened. "What a lovely compliment, Maria. Especially since I know how carefully you plan your displays at the Stocking Stitch. But are you sure my work will be a good fit?"

"Without a doubt," Maria said promptly. "Your tapestries will be an inspiration for my customers."

Isabella flushed, pleased beyond measure. "I would love to have my work in your shop," she said with heartfelt warmth. "But I can't help but wonder if you're hoping our connection through the Stocking Stitch will bring Roberto and me together."

"Much as I'd love to see that happen, Isabella, I've given up hoping matchmaking efforts might succeed with Roberto," Maria said, her expressive face serious. "I suspect he gave his heart away at some point in the past. I'm afraid he's never gotten over whoever the woman was, and may never do so."

"I'm so sorry, Maria." Isabella instinctively reached out, her hand closing in swift sympathy over Maria's where it clutched her purse.

"No need to apologize, my dear," Maria said, her smile wistful. "If I thought matchmaking for Roberto would work, I'd try. But as it is…" Her voice trailed off and she sighed. "Be that as it may," she said determinedly after a brief moment. "I'm delighted you're agreeable to my proposal. When can you drop by the shop and discuss the details?"

The two women spent several moments arranging a date before Maria was called away by Lily Fortune.

"I need to speak to you in private," Lily murmured. She glanced about the crowded room before catching Maria's arm and walking with her to the relative quiet of a corner.

Intrigued, Maria went willingly.

"What is it?" she asked when they had a small degree of privacy.

"I wanted to ask if you've learned anything new from the investigators about the fire that burned down the restaurant," Lily said softly.

"Not that I'm aware of," Maria said, just as quietly. "But José stays in touch with the fire department and asked the chief to contact us if there are any new developments. I'm assuming he'll be in touch when he has any information. Why? Have you heard something?"

Lily sighed. "I can't help feeling the fires at Red and the Double Crown are related. I received a second anonymous note that said, 'This one wasn't an accident either.'"

"You didn't tell me about the notes." Maria caught her breath. "What did the first one say?"

Lily glanced around, assuring there was no one near enough to hear their whispered conversation. "'One of the Fortunes is not who you think,'" she quoted.

Maria frowned. "That's terribly vague. What do you suppose it means?"

"I have no idea." Lily's face was strained. "At first I thought someone was planning to blackmail the family. But then the fires happened—and the second note arrived." She bit her lip. "I'm afraid someone is going to be seriously hurt."

"We can't let that happen," Maria said with emphasis. "It's a miracle someone wasn't injured already in one of the two fires."

"My family has hired Cindy's son, Ross, to investigate. He wants me to call in the police, but I dread the publicity that would surely follow."

"I can't say I blame you," Maria agreed. "But you mustn't take chances, Lily. You live alone out on the Double Crown. I think you should hire protection."

"You mean an armed guard of some sort?" Lily asked, clearly startled by the suggestion.

"Absolutely," Maria said stoutly. "What if this anonymous person decides to set fire to someone's house next? And with you living alone…well, it's just too dangerous."

Lily shook her head. "No, I refuse to give in to intimidation. I have staff at the ranch and I'll warn them to be more alert for anything that seems unusual. But I'm not going to let this person, whomever it is, terrorize me."

"Then promise me you'll be careful, very careful," Maria admonished.

"I will." Lily smiled at her friend. "And if I'm afraid for any reason to stay alone, I promise I'll show up on your doorstep, bags in hand, and ask to use your guest room."

"José and I will be delighted to have you," Maria said promptly, and enfolded Lily in a warm hug.

As Maria and Lily made plans, Nick and Charlene were scraping tomato and guacamole off Jessie's blue jumper.

"I'll take her to the restroom and sluice the rest of it off her face and hands," Nick said. "Are you okay here with these two?"

Charlene glanced at Jenny and Jackie. They were chortling, waving their white linen napkins and stretching to reach a bowl of guacamole and chips just out of reach.

"We're fine." She laughed and moved the green guacamole across the table, out of Jenny's reach. "If they try to eat the table, I'll call 9-1-1."

Nick grinned, laugh lines crinkling at the corners of his eyes. "You might want to put that on speed dial."

He headed for the bathroom, glancing over his shoulder just before he left the room. Two of Maria's daughters and their husbands were standing next to Charlene, talking animatedly.

There was a lot to be said on occasion for a large family, he thought.

When he left the rest room, Jessie's face and hands scrubbed clean and dried, he'd barely entered the dining room when his cousin, Frannie, stopped him.

"Nick!" She caught him in a warm hug. He returned the affectionate embrace one-armed, keeping Jessie from being sandwiched between them by tucking her higher against his shoulder.

"Hey, Frannie." He smiled down at her. "Are you solo tonight or is Lloyd here?"

"Not only Lloyd, but also Josh and his girlfriend, Lyndsey," she said. "You look better than ever, Nick. What have you been doing with yourself?"

Given that sexual frustration rode him hard nearly every hour of the day, Nick was taken aback at Frannie's comment. "Must be my girls," he said, retrieving his balance with quick aplomb. He chucked Jessie under the chin and she grinned at him. "Is that true, Jessie?"

"Your girls?" Frannie repeated, clearly stunned. "I didn't know you had children, Nick. When did this happen?"

"I'm their temporary guardian. This is Jessie and those…" he pointed across the room "…are Jessie's identical sisters, Jackie and Jenny."

Frannie stared at him, eyes wide. "Tell me how this happened."

By the time Nick repeated his story, Frannie was tickling Jessie's fingers, trying to get her to accept a hug. But Jessie clung to Nick, although she giggled when Frannie made a comical face.

"...And that's the short version of the whole story," Nick concluded. "You've done the parenting thing, Frannie, do you have any expert advice for me?"

Frannie's smile faded. "I'm afraid I'm the last person you'd want advice from, Nick. Neither Lloyd nor I approve of Lyndsey, our son's latest girlfriend. I think Josh is too young to be so involved. I wish they would both date other people and gain more experience before they get serious. But they're so intense about each other."

"If I remember correctly," Nick said gently, "I think you were around Josh's age when you married Lloyd, weren't you?"

"Exactly," Frannie said grimly. "I don't want Josh to make the same mistakes I did." Her gaze swept the big room, stopping abruptly.

Nick half-turned to see what had caught her attention and located Josh, deep in conversation with a pretty young blond girl. She was petite and looked almost fragile.

"I take it that's Lyndsey?"

"Yes." Frannie sighed. She looked at Nick. "Be glad you're only the temporary guardian of the triplets, Nick, and won't be spending their teenage years sleepless and worried about the choices they make."

Someone called her name and she excused herself

to hurry off before Nick could respond. He watched her go, wondering what, exactly, she thought Josh was up to with Lyndsey.

He hoped to God there wasn't a pregnancy involved. After caring for the triplets, he was convinced no teenager should have babies.

Maybe not even twenty-year-olds should have kids.

He looked at Jessie, bent to kiss the top of her silky curls, and shifted her higher against his shoulder.

"No dating for you until you're forty," he told her sternly. "And maybe not even then. Remember, celibacy is a good concept."

She laughed, burbled nonsensically, and bopped him on the chin with a little fist.

Pleased she seemed to understand his lecture, Nick wove his way around diners toward the table where Charlene waited with Jackie and Jenny.

As Nick moved to join Charlene, José Mendoza was deep in conversation with Ross Fortune in one of the smaller, table-filled rooms just off the big main dining room.

"I'm convinced the fire here at the restaurant wasn't an accident," José said forcefully. He glanced around, lowering his voice as he continued. "We installed a state-of-the-art sprinkler system not four months before the fire and the smoke alarms are checked each week. There's no way a fire could have burned out of control and destroyed the building unless someone tampered with the protection systems."

"And used a powerful accelerant," Ross commented, eyes narrowing in thought.

"Probably." José nodded decisively. "Although I can't figure out why anyone would want to burn down the restaurant."

"I'm working on the theory that the two fires might be connected—the one here at Red and the barn out at the Double Crown," Ross said, lowering his voice to keep from being overheard.

José looked taken aback. "What makes you think they're connected?"

Ross scanned the clusters of people, chatting and laughing. "I'd like to show you something." He took a note from his pocket and handed it over.

The older man unfolded the paper, read the single line and frowned. He looked up at Ross. "'This one wasn't an accident either,'" he quoted. "Where did you get this? What does it mean?"

"It's a copy of a note that was slipped into Lily's pocket after the fire at the Double Crown. She doesn't have a clue who put it there, nor who wrote it. But it certainly suggests the two fires are connected." Ross took the note from José and tucked it back into his jacket pocket. "I was hoping you might shed some light as to who might have a grudge against your family and the Fortunes."

José frowned, his eyes narrowing as he considered the question.

"The Mendoza and Fortune families have been close for a long time," he said after a moment. "But I can't imagine anyone would want to hurt my family this way, nor how it could be connected to the Fortunes."

"The two families are more than friends—your daughter, Gloria, married Jack Fortune. Do you know of any disgruntled boyfriends who might want to get back at you because of the marriage?"

"No." José's reply was swift and certain. "I can't think of anyone angry enough about their wedding, nor about any other situation with our families, to plan this sort of revenge."

"No disgruntled employees or business deals gone bad?" Ross prodded.

Once again, José shook his head. "The only mutual ties between our families are our long-standing friendship and the marriage between Gloria and Jack. I don't see how either of those could drive someone to blackmail or arson."

"Which makes me wonder if there might be some other link between your two families. Something we're not seeing," Ross mused.

"What's this about blackmail and arson?" Roberto Mendoza interrupted, joining them. He listened as his father quickly filled him in.

"This is a hell of a situation," he said when José finished his narrative.

"Yeah," Ross agreed.

"How close are you to finding out who did this?" Roberto asked grimly.

"No way of telling." Ross shrugged. "I still have people to interview and leads to follow."

Ross continued to speak but Roberto didn't hear

him. Distracted, his gaze was focused through the archway and across the dining room, his dark face solemn and intent.

Across the busy main room of Red Restaurant, hidden in the shadows, two figures watched the chattering, laughing groups of celebrants. Frowns of dislike twisted each face into matching expressions of irritation.

"Despite all this celebrating, I have it on good authority the Fortunes are concerned and taking the threats seriously."

"They seem to have changed their attitude since the second fire—which was a brilliant move, if I say so myself. If this were a chess game, I'd say we're very close to declaring checkmate." The voice held satisfaction.

"Yes." The response was smug, with a hint of gloating. "The Fortunes think they're so smart and powerful. Well, we'll see who wins in the end."

"I don't doubt the Fortunes will lose this game. Perhaps we should step up the plan? Raise the stakes—rattle the Fortunes even more. We have to make sure our position is secure."

"Are you saying the measures we've taken up to this point haven't been sufficiently threatening?" The words were laced with hostility.

"No, of course not." The response was instant and faintly irritated. "The Fortune family's sense of well-being has clearly been damaged. I'm merely suggesting it might be wise to push them even harder."

"I see your point."

"Excellent." The word oozed satisfaction. "I'm sure if we decide to plan another…incident, we can execute it every bit as well as the prior ones."

"Absolutely." Conviction and a bone-chilling malice underscored the word.

Nick and Charlene left the party early, but even so, the hour was late for the triplets and past their bedtime. The three nodded off in their car seats on the drive home.

By the time Charlene and Nick carried the girls into the house, changed diapers and tucked the babies into their pajamas, the fractious girls were overtired and too awake to fall back to sleep.

"Why don't I take Jessie and Jenny downstairs," Nick said. "I'll turn on the music and walk the floor with them while you rock Jenny up here. When she falls asleep, you can put her in her crib. With luck, one of my two will be asleep by then and we can each deal with one."

"Good plan," Charlene agreed. She was settling into the rocking chair as Nick left the room. A few moments later, Norah Jones's husky voice floated up the stairwell. Charlene contemplated switching on the audio sensor in the bedroom to activate the nearest speaker. But the music was loud enough without the added sound, so she rejected the idea and cuddled Jenny, singing along with Norah Jones.

Jenny squirmed and fussed, unhappy, frustrated, and much too tired to settle. Finally, her eyelashes drifted lower and her breathing slowed. Five minutes later, Jenny's sturdy little body had gone boneless in Charlene's arms.

Rising from the rocker, Charlene carried her across the room and laid her in her crib, tucking her blanket over her. Jenny sighed and curled onto her side, dragging her blanket with her to cuddle the satin binding against her cheek.

Charlene stood over the crib for a moment, struck by the deep sense of contentment the moment held. Then she headed downstairs.

In the living room, Nick walked back and forth with a baby against each shoulder. Jackie and Jessie were still awake, their cheeks stained with tears, but their eyes were half-closed and their blankets hugged close.

"How's it going?" Charlene said softly.

"Another few minutes and they'll be out for the count." Nick tipped his head to look at Jackie, whose face was nearly hidden behind her blanket in the curve of his shoulder. "If you'll take her, I'll walk Jessie for a little longer."

They managed the handoff without rousing either child, and barely a half hour later they had tucked the two sleeping little girls into their cribs, then tiptoed quietly out of the room.

"Well…" Charlene tucked her hair behind one ear and gestured vaguely. "It's been a long day."

"Yeah, it has." Nick shoved his hands in his slacks pockets. "Thanks for helping out with the girls. I really appreciate it."

She couldn't read his face, although instinct told

her there was suppressed emotion behind his polite remote expression.

"I was glad to do it. And it was a pleasure meeting your family—and the Mendozas and all their friends." She smiled, willing him to let whatever he was feeling break through the impassive facade. "I enjoyed myself—and I think the girls did too."

A faint smile curved his mouth, lightening his expression and easing the hard lines of his face. "They would have enjoyed themselves more if we'd let them climb on top of the table and play in the guacamole bowls."

"I'm sure they would," she said wryly. "Fortunately for the rest of the guests, we managed to restrain them."

His smile faded, his eyes hooded as he looked at her with an intensity she felt as surely as if he'd stroked his hand over her skin.

"Well…" she said, suddenly strung with nerves. "I'll see you in the morning, then. Good night."

She reached her bedroom door before he responded.

"Good night."

The simple words held dark undertones that shivered up her spine like a caress. She didn't look back, only slipped quickly inside and closed the door with the distinct impression that she'd just avoided danger.

Living in the same house with Nick Fortune was fraught with temptation. And she was a woman who had little resistance when it came to the undeniably handsome bachelor.

As she'd learned such a short time ago. During that mind-numbing kiss in the kitchen.

Nick hadn't spent his bachelor years avoiding women, she knew. The man could kiss. Just the memory of his mouth on hers made her toes curl and her heart pound.

Since she had very few defenses against Nick, she could only hope his commitment to keep them at arm's length while they worked together held fast.

Because she wasn't at all sure she could withstand him if he crooked his finger and smiled at her to lure her closer.

Chapter Eight

Both Nick and Charlene were hyperaware that their time with the triplets was running out. Much too quickly the days flew by, and all too soon the much-awaited telephone call was received. The babies' aunt and uncle had arrived, checked into a local hotel and wanted to arrange a time to come to the house.

Fortunately, it was Sunday morning and the timing was right. Nick was home, stretched out on the living-room floor while he stacked blocks with the triplets. The girls happily knocked them over as soon as he built a tower, then crawled after the rolling blocks to toss them back at him. Charlene sat on the sofa, smiling at their antics. She jumped nervously when the doorbell rang, her gaze flying to meet Nick's.

"You stay here with the girls. I'll get the door."

Wordlessly, she nodded and Nick left the room. She heard the door open and the quick murmur of voices. A moment later, Nick ushered a man and woman into the living room.

"Charlene, this is Lana Berland and her husband, John," Nick said as they approached. He bent and lifted Jackie into his arms. "This is Jackie. Charlene's holding Jenny—and Jessie is trying to chew the remote control for the stereo system. Jessie, give me that." He bent his knees and scooped the little girl up to perch on his arm. She instantly patted his face and burbled a stream of unintelligible chatter. "Yes, I know, honey, but you can't chew the remote. If you ate it, you'd wind up with plastic rash somewhere."

The three adults, watching him, burst into laughter at the same time, breaking the awkwardness of the moment.

"They're such beautiful babies," Lana said, her eyes welling as she looked at them. "They look so much like their parents. They have Amy's eyes and Stan's black hair."

"Would you like to hold Jessie?" Charlene asked.

"Oh, yes, please." Lana eagerly held out her arms but the little girl clung to Charlene, burying her face against Charlene's neck.

"Perhaps she needs a bit more time to get used to you," Charlene suggested, seeing Lana's stricken expression. "Won't you have a seat?" She gestured at the sofa and perched on the chair with Jessie when Lana sat on the nearby end of the leather couch.

"They're shy with new people," Nick comented, taking a seat on the far end of the sofa with Jackie and Jenny.

"They couldn't remember us," Lana said, glancing at John. "We were back in the States shortly after they were born, but then we left for Africa. We'd planned to return in December to spend Christmas with Stan and Amy this year…" Her voice broke and she faltered.

John sat beside her and took her hand, threading her fingers through his.

"It was a huge shock to hear about Stan and Amy, as I'm sure you understand," he said quietly. "Lana hasn't had time to come to terms with it."

"I understand," Nick said, the bones of his face suddenly more prominent, his jaw tight. "I'm not sure how long it's supposed to take, but a week certainly isn't enough time."

"No," Lana said softly, her eyes filled with compassion and empathy.

"I understand you two were stranded by flooding," Nick said, abruptly changing the conversation. "How long were you cut off?"

Lana and John seemed relieved at Nick's steering the conversation away from the tragedy that had brought them all together. For the next half hour, they chatted companionably about the flooding and the political situation in the area of southern Africa where Lana and John had lived and worked. They also discussed the triplets as Nick and Charlene related episodes that had all four adults laughing.

When Nick told them about the girls' difficulty sleeping through the night and using music to quiet them, Lana clapped her hands with appreciation.

"What a brilliant solution," she said with admiration. "I wouldn't be surprised if Amy and Stan used some of the same music."

"I don't know if they've always been little night owls or if they were upset by the drastic changes in their lives," Nick said. "The court temporarily placed them with a foster mother in Amarillo for several days after the accident before I picked them up and brought them here. It has to be confusing for them— so I guess we shouldn't complain about their not sleeping at first."

"That brings up something John and I wanted to talk to you about," Lana said. She looked at her husband, then back at Nick. "We spent most of the plane ride home discussing how to make the transition with the least impact on the girls."

Charlene saw Nick's body go taut. She doubted Lana or John noticed, but she recognized the telltale signs. She too braced herself.

"As you said, their lives have been terribly disrupted already and by switching their home and caretakers, yet again, we're going to upset their schedules. We thought perhaps the best way might be to ease them into the transition—by having them remain with you for several days, perhaps a week, while John and I visit daily. That would give the girls time to grow accustomed to our being around and allow us to ease into their lives. If the change isn't quite as abrupt, hopefully the stress of transition for the girls will be less when they come to live with us full-time."

Some of the tenseness eased out of Nick's body. "Sounds like a reasonable plan." His gaze met Charlene's for a moment. "I've wondered whether they'll be okay with another sudden shift in their living arrangements. I'm sure Charlene has too."

"Yes, I have," Charlene acknowledged, swept with relief that Lana and John's first concern was for the triplets' welfare. Something cold and scared inside her chest eased and she drew a deep breath. "Will you be taking them back to Amarillo?"

"We haven't had time to make definite plans, but that seems the most reasonable choice. We're temporarily without jobs, or a home—my sister's estate is left to the girls under our guardianship and their house in Amarillo is available, of course." She glanced at her husband and once again, he squeezed her hand comfortingly. "John and I don't have any personal ties there, now that Amy and Stan are gone." She blinked back tears.

"We don't have to decide all the details right this minute, sweetheart," John murmured, slipping an arm around his wife's shoulders.

Jessie chattered, squirming. Charlene shifted her grip on the little girl.

"What is it?" she asked before she realized Jackie and Jenny were also fussing. She glanced at her watch. "It's nearly twelve—time for the girls' lunch." Her gaze met Nick's. "Would you like me to feed them while you discuss arrangements with Lana and John?"

"I think we'll have time to work out details over the next few days. Why don't we all go into the kitchen and make lunch." Nick surged to his feet, bringing Jackie and Jenny with him. "Might as well start getting the girls more comfortable with their aunt and uncle." His lips quirked in a grin. "There's nothing like dodging strained carrots to bring a one-year-old closer to an adult—especially when one of the triplets starts and the other two join in because they think it's hilariously funny. It's a real bonding experience." He lifted an eyebrow at John. "Have any objections to getting applesauce in your hair?"

"None," John said promptly, his eyes twinkling.

"Good." Nick waved the three adults ahead of him. "We need to find something to cover you with, Lana, or the dress you're wearing is going to have food all over it by the time the girls are done eating."

Lana laughed. "Looks like I need an apron."

"Melissa has one in the kitchen—I'll get it for you," Charlene said as they all trooped out of the living room and down the hall.

During the following days, Nick and Charlene had time to get to know Lana and John. Observing their interaction with the triplets put to rest any lingering fears as to how well the couple would cope as parents.

On the last night the triplets would spend at Nick's home, Charlene couldn't fall asleep. She tried reading a new novel, but was too restless to sink into the story. Giving up, she put the book aside and booted up her laptop. Her efforts to focus on updating her resume and making job-search lists were no more successful than her earlier attempts to read.

She found herself staring blankly at the screen. *This is probably the last night I'll spend here,* she thought, her gaze leaving the laptop to move around the comfortable room.

And the last night I'll sleep in Nick's house.

Would she see him again after the triplets left with Lana and John?

Probably not, she acknowledged, her heart twisting with regret and pain. Her job would end when Nick no longer needed her help with the babies.

No more shared laughter with Nick over the babies' antics. No more shared outings, like their walk to the coffee shop or the evening at Red.

And no more unexpected hot kisses with early-morning coffee.

Tears clogged the back of her throat. She'd never know what those kisses might have led to—Nick was clearly determined not to get involved with her. She had to focus on saying goodbye to the triplets—and then move on.

She closed her files, shut down the laptop and moved it to the bedside table before she switched off the lamp. She fluffed her pillow, tugged the sheet higher, and determinedly closed her eyes.

A half hour later, she checked the digital clock for the third time and groaned aloud. The luminescent dial told her the time was twelve-thirty in the a.m.

Frustrated, she stared at the ceiling and tried counting sheep. Their woolly shapes quickly morphed into babies with black curls and sparkling blue eyes. All of them looked exactly like Jackie, Jenny and Jessie.

Muttering, she pulled her pillow over her head and tried not to picture adorable laughing triplets.

The muffled sound of music penetrated the soft down-filled pillow. Clearly, the audio system had activated in the triplets' room.

Perhaps she shouldn't be glad she would have this one last chance to check on them in the dark hours of night, she thought as she left her bedroom and crossed the hall. But somehow, she couldn't regret that one of them had wakened.

The door to their bedroom was ajar and she slipped inside noiselessly, only to halt abruptly.

Nick stood next to Jenny's crib, the little girl cradled against his chest. His head was bent, lips touching the crown of her silky curls as he gently rocked her in his arms.

Charlene's heart caught and tears welled. Clearly, she wasn't the only one having a hard time letting the girls go.

Unwilling to intrude on Nick's privacy, she turned to leave.

His head lifted and he glanced over his shoulder.

She stopped, held by the intensity in his dark eyes, shadowed further by the dim night-light.

"I didn't know you were here," she said softly, whispering so as not to wake the babies. "I heard the music and thought I'd make sure the girls were okay."

Nick nodded and carefully lowered Jenny into her crib. She stirred, curling on her side on the white sheet with its pattern of pink bunnies in flowered hats.

He tucked her blanket closer. She clutched it tightly and sighed, her eyes closed, her limbs sprawling as she fell more deeply asleep.

Nick joined Charlene at the door and motioned her outside, pausing to pull the door nearly closed.

"If I'd known you were here, I wouldn't have interrupted," she whispered.

"Don't worry about it." He ran his hand over his hair, further rumpling it. "I didn't mind checking on Jenny."

"The music didn't put her back to sleep?" Charlene asked, wondering if the little girl was coming down with something.

Nick shrugged, his expression wry. "It might have, but she saw me when I looked in. I thought she might wake the others, so I picked her up."

"Ah." Charlene nodded. She suspected Nick may have had the same reaction she'd had to hearing the music click on and used it as an excuse for a quiet moment with Jenny. "It's hard to believe they'll be gone tomorrow."

"Yeah." His eyes turned somber. "It is."

"I'm going to miss them."

He nodded. "When all this started, I never thought I'd wish I could keep them, but somehow I do."

Charlene fought the onslaught of tears and lost.

Despite her best efforts, her eyes filled, then over-flowed with tears. They spilled down her cheeks.

"Hey," he said softly, moving closer, narrowing the space between them to mere inches. He cupped her face, brushing the pads of his thumbs over the tears dampening her cheeks. "Don't cry."

"I can't help it," she managed to get out past a throat clogged with emotion. "I know I shouldn't have grown so attached, but I couldn't help myself. I didn't plan to," she shrugged helplessly. "It just happened."

Nick cupped her shoulders and gently urged her forward, tucking her against his chest and wrapping his arms around her. "I know," he said soothingly, his chin resting against the crown of her head. "If it's any comfort, I feel the same way. God knows I never thought I'd get used to having three babies around. They cause total chaos—there's food in crazy places I can't reach in my kitchen because they threw it there. I hate changing dirty diapers. And staggering through ten-hour workdays after a couple hours of sleep in the beginning sure as hell wasn't fun. Despite all that, they somehow sneaked under my radar when I wasn't looking. They've grown on me. I actually like the little tyrants."

Charlene accepted the comfort of his embrace without questioning, giving in to the need to be held. His hands moved in soothing circles on her back, the solid warmth of his body supporting her, and her sobs gradually slowed.

She calmed. And was instantly too aware of Nick.

The hall was nearly dark, only faintly lit by cool, silvery moonlight, filtered through the leafy tree outside the window at the far end.

The arms that held her were warm and bare—so was the muscled chest she lay against. Her thighs were pressed against his hair-roughened ones.

She realized with a sudden rush of heat that Nick wasn't wearing the pajama bottoms he'd pulled on in the earlier days when the triplets often got him out of bed in the middle of the night. He was wearing boxers.

Her clothing was just as minimal. The thin tank top she wore over cotton sleep shorts may as well have been made of air for all the barrier it provided between her skin and his.

Her breath hitched. Her heart beat faster, driven by the slow excitement that coiled in her abdomen and spread outward to her fingers and toes. Every inch of her was much too aware that this was Nick who held her—and she wanted him.

She heard his breathing change, felt the subtle tension in the muscled body surrounding her.

"Charlene," his voice rasped, deeper, huskier.

"Yes?" She tilted her head back and looked up at him. His mouth had a sensuous fullness, his eyes slumberous between half-lowered lids.

"You're fired," he said roughly.

"What?" She blinked, disoriented.

"I'm fresh out of self-control. And we can't make love if you're working for me. When we wake up in the morning, you're hired again. But for tonight," he brushed the pad of his thumb over her bottom lip. "It's just us."

"Are you sure about this?" She didn't want a repeat of their moment in the kitchen when she'd been swept away, only to crash, bruised and hurt, when he told her he regretted kissing her.

"I'm sure," he muttered. "The question is, sugar, are you? 'Cause if you aren't, you're fast running out of time to tell me."

Knowing this may very well be the last night she'd spend in his house and perhaps the last time she'd have a chance to be with him, Charlene didn't hesitate. With swift decision, she met his gaze and gave the only answer possible.

"I'm sure."

Instantly he crushed her mouth under his for one fierce kiss, then bent and swung her into his arms.

Like the hallway, his bedroom was lit by silvery moonlight. He set her on her feet, her legs slowly sliding against his, and threaded his hands through her hair, tilting her face up to kiss her again. The kiss scorched her nerve endings, the slow, thorough exploration of her mouth sending shivers of excitement through her. When he finally lifted his lips, her knees were weak. She clutched his biceps for support when he eased back, his hands settling at her waist, thumbs stroking beneath the hem of her tank top.

"You're wearing too many clothes," he rasped, his voice thick with arousal.

She licked her lips. "So are you," she murmured,

her gaze fastened on the sensual twist of his mouth as he smiled briefly.

"I can fix that." His hands moved, carrying her top upward and baring her torso. He pulled the cotton shirt free of her hair and tossed it behind him.

The moonlight fell across his face, highlighting his intent expression as he stared at her, his eyes half-lidded. Charlene's breasts swelled under his gaze, heavy and sensitive. Her knees nearly buckled when he palmed her, stroking his thumbs over the sensitive tips.

She clung tighter, gasping when he bent his head and took her nipple in his mouth. Her head spun as he licked her, the warm, wet cavern of his mouth soothing the tender flesh.

He slipped his hands beneath the waistband of her shorts and pushed them down and off before his arms wrapped around her to pull her flush against him.

"Please. Please, Nick," she murmured, nearly frantic with the need to have him closer.

He muttered what sounded like a curse and, one-handed, shoved his boxers to the floor.

The covers were tossed to the foot of the king-size bed and Nick lowered her to the sheet, following her down.

His weight blanketed her from shoulders to thighs, his big body crowding hers. He levered himself up on his forearms, the hard angles of his hips tight against the softer cove of hers, and bent his head to take her mouth. She shuddered, her hands clutching his shoulders as she welcomed the urgent thrust of his tongue. Taut with excitement, she lifted to press her breasts against his chest, shifting against him, the drag of bare skin against his hard, sleek muscles ratcheting up the tension that gripped her. He kissed her mouth, chin, then trailed his lips down the curve of her throat. The warm weight of his hand settled at her waist. His thumb grazed the small hollow of her belly button. Then his fingers moved higher, over her midriff, until the backs of his fingers brushed the underside of her breast.

The harsh intake of his breath was audible, his hard body going taut.

Impatient, Charlene hooked one leg over his, her calf sliding over the hair-roughened back of his thigh, urging him closer.

His mouth took hers at the same moment his hand closed over her breast and his hips rocked against hers. Heated moments later, Charlene was frantic with need.

He shifted away from her to don protection, then nudged against her center and she wrapped her arms and legs around him, opening herself as he groaned and thrust home.

Charlene came awake slowly, drifting upward through layers of sleep. Heat branded her back, thighs and calves. Something heavy lay across her waist. She shifted, stretching lazily, her toes brushing hair-roughened muscles.

Her eyes popped open and she stared blankly at the bar of early morning light that lay across the end of the bed. For one baffled moment, she tried to understand why her bedspread was now a deep cobalt blue when it had been white and green last night.

Memory washed over her and her eyes widened.

This wasn't her bed—or her bedroom.

It was Nick's. Carefully, she turned her head on the pillow to look over her shoulder at the man sharing the bed.

Nick's body—his bare, naked body—was curled against hers, branding her from shoulderblades to toes. And it was his arm that lay like a possessive bar over her waist, his fingers curled loosely over her ribcage, just below her breast.

A soft smile curved her mouth. There was such an overwhelming sense of rightness—waking with Nick wrapped around her. For several long moments she lay still, basking in the sheer pleasure and the memories of the night they'd spent making love.

Nick was an amazing lover. She should have known he would be by that sizzling first kiss in the kitchen, she thought.

Her gaze drifted lazily past Nick's broad shoulder and landed on the alarm clock.

Her eyes widened.

Good Lord, was that the right time?

The triplets would be awake before long and Lana and John were picking them up today. There were a million and one things to accomplish before they arrived.

With a last lingering look at Nick's sprawled body, Charlene slipped out of his bed. Catching up her top and sleep shorts from where they lay in a heap on the floor, she stole silently out of his room to take a shower in her own bathroom.

"They're here," Nick announced, his voice carrying up the stairs.

Charlene drew a deep breath.

"You okay, honey?" LouAnn's raspy voice held warm concern.

"Yes." Charlene glanced sideways and found the older woman's face soft with compassion.

"It's not easy saying goodbye when you've become attached to little ones," LouAnn said. "I've had to do it a time or two myself." She picked up Jessie, balancing her on one bony hip. "I've never been sorry I had the experience, though, once I had a few weeks to cry my eyes out and get used to them being gone."

Charlene laughed. Granted, it was more of a half laugh, half sob, but LouAnn's blunt and thoroughly practical observation was enough to get her past the emotional moment.

"Thanks, LouAnn."

The older woman winked at her. "Don't worry. I expect you'll be having babies of your own one of these days, soon enough. I've seen Nick look at you, and if ever a man is head-over-heels, it's Nick. I'd bet my last dollar on it."

Charlene didn't reply, busying herself with picking up Jackie and Jenny. She didn't want to think about what Nick did or didn't feel—she'd spent too many hours over the last days agonizing over him. And making love last night had sent her emotions cart-wheeling out of control. She simply couldn't think about Nick now—not if she was going to say goodbye to the triplets with any semblance of dignity.

"There you are." Nick met them halfway up the stairs and lifted Jenny out of her arms. "You should have waited—I'd have carried one of them downstairs."

"Not to worry, we managed." She avoided his gaze and looked over his shoulder at the couple standing in the foyer. "Hello, Lana, John."

"Good morning," they responded.

A mountain of luggage, three diaper bags stuffed to overflowing and boxes with toys poking out of the top filled one corner of the foyer.

Lana held out her arms and Jackie went happily, chattering away as her aunt listened intently and nodded.

The interaction between the two was bittersweet for Charlene—comforting because Jackie clearly felt at home with her aunt, but saddening because she left Charlene's arms so willingly.

"We have some good news," John said.

"What's that?" Nick asked, sitting Jenny on the floor with a stuffed green dragon.

"Do you want to tell them, Lana?" John grinned at his wife.

For the first time since descending the stairs, Charlene noticed Lana wore an air of suppressed excitement.

"Yes, let me." Lana nodded emphatically, beaming at Nick, then Charlene. "We have fabulous news.

John has been offered a job at the Fortune Foundation and we're not going back to Amarillo—we're going to stay right here in Red Rock. And we found the loveliest house not more than a mile or so from here. So the babies won't be going far," she ended with a lilting laugh. "Isn't that wonderful? I was feeling so badly, knowing we were taking them so far away from you both and you wouldn't be able to see them regularly. But now we'll practically be neighbors, so anytime you want to drop in and visit the girls, you can."

Nick looked as stunned as Charlene felt. Then he smiled, a broad grin that lit his face.

"That's great news."

"Yes, absolutely wonderful," Charlene added.

"This deserves a celebration," Nick declared. "Come into the kitchen—there's a bottle of champagne in the fridge. I promise I won't give either of you more than a swallow or two, since you'll be dealing with the triplets today."

They trooped into the kitchen, babies and all, and while Nick took out champagne and Charlene found flutes in the cupboard, Lana and John filled in the details.

"I'll be managing a project to establish an after-school enrichment program for underprivileged kids in San Antonio," John said as Nick handed around flutes with the bubbling gold liquid.

"I'm familiar with it," Nick said. "I worked up projection figures for the costs. The proposal for services was impressive."

"The work is tailor-made for John," Lana put in, clearly elated. "His primary interest has always been in programs that enhance the lives of children."

Nick winked at her and lifted his glass. "With the triplets in your house and heading up the Foundation's new project, I'd say he's hit the jackpot."

Laughter filled the kitchen, glasses were raised, and it was an hour later before Lana glanced at her watch.

"Look at the time, John. I didn't realize it was so late." She stood, balancing Jessie on her hip. "By the time we get the girls' things loaded, drive to the house and unload, it will be nearly time for the girls' naps." She tapped a forefinger on the tip of Jessie's upturned nose. "We don't want to start off on the wrong foot."

"Agreed."

Since the new house was so close, Nick insisted he help transport and unload the triplets' belongings.

Much too soon, Charlene found herself standing at the curb, waving good-bye as the two vehicles drove away down the street.

She went inside, the silence seeming to close about her when she shut the door. She walked into the kitchen to wash the crystal flutes and return them to their shelf. After wiping down the marble countertop, she glanced once more around the kitchen and then headed upstairs.

It was time to pack—and leave.

Chapter Nine

"What are you doing?"

Charlene stiffened, steeling herself before she turned. Nick stood in the open doorway, frowning at her.

"I'm packing." She walked to the closet and slipped the little black cocktail dress off its hanger, folding it as she returned to the bed and the open suitcase.

"I can see that," he said impatiently. "Why?"

She tucked the dress into the bag before she looked at him. "Because it's easier to carry clothes in suitcases, of course."

"Where are you going?"

"I'm not sure yet." She opened a dresser drawer,

removed several T-shirts and laid them on top of the black dress. "Now that the girls are with Lana and John, my job here is finished."

"Yeah, I suppose it is."

Charlene felt her heart drop and realized she'd been holding her breath, hoping he'd tell her to stay. The scowl on his face, however, was convincing evidence that he had no interest in prolonging her time. She forced a smile. "I'll be out of your way in another half hour and you'll have your house to yourself again. I'm sure you'll be glad you can return to peace and quiet," she said as she crossed the room to fetch her toiletries from the bathroom.

"Not likely," he muttered.

"I beg your pardon?" She paused, sure she must have misheard him.

"I hope you've been comfortable here," he gestured at the room, not directly answering her question.

"Oh, yes." She looked about her, knowing she would miss the way the early-morning sun shone through her window each morning, throwing a leafy pattern across the bed from the tree just outside. And she'd miss the well-planned cozy kitchen downstairs, and Nick's state-of-the-art coffeemaker. She drew in a deep breath and managed another vague, polite smile in his direction. She didn't look at him for fear the tears pressing behind her eyes would escape her rigid control and spill over. "You have a lovely home, Nick. Anyone would enjoy spending time here."

"The hell with this," he ground out.

Startled, Charlene switched her gaze from the suitcase to Nick and found him stalking toward her.

"You can't leave." His face was taut. He caught her shoulders in his big hands and held her. "I don't want you to leave."

"You don't?" Charlene was stunned, too afraid to hope, even more afraid that she might leap to conclusions. She needed him to spell out exactly what he meant. "Why?"

"Because I want you to marry me, live with me, have babies with me."

"But…" Charlene's brain spun, trying to absorb this sudden switch. "But you said you never planned to marry. Or have children. You said you couldn't imagine having a family—that you thought Stan and Amy were crazy to pick you to take care of their girls."

"I said a lot of stupid things," Nick said with disgust. "The only reason I was a confirmed bachelor is because I hadn't met you."

"Really?" Charlene's eyes misted. "That's a lovely thing to say."

"I should have said it before." His hands tightened. "I wanted you the day I met you but I told myself all I felt was lust. And you worked for me. I've never crossed the line and slept with an employee." His eyes darkened, his hands stroking down her back to settle at her waist and tug her forward to rest against him. "I couldn't stop myself last night."

"Neither could I," she admitted.

"Darr and J.R. knew I was in love with you. I've known for a while, but it took seeing you packing your suitcase to make me say the words out loud."

"I don't mind." Charlene cupped his face in her palms. "As long as you said it." Her words eased the tension from his face.

He bent his head and brushed his mouth over hers. "Now it's your turn."

Charlene slipped her arms around his neck and went up on tiptoe. "I love you too," she murmured, her lips barely touching his before he leaned back, preventing her from reaching him. Her mouth skimmed his chin.

He bent his head and nuzzled her neck. "That's the best news I heard all day."

"Mmm." Distracted by the movement of his warm mouth against her skin, she was having difficulty following their conversation. She tilted her chin as he nudged aside her shirt. Dazed, she realized she hadn't even felt him unbutton the blue cotton.

He smiled, his mouth branding an amused curve on her skin, and then he lifted his head to look down at her.

"Just remember when we talk about this later—you agreed."

He caught the edges of her shirt. Buttons popped as he ripped it open and stripped it off her shoulders. He shoved the suitcase off the bed and it hit the floor. Charlene barely noticed that the contents spilled out in a fan of color against the pale-green carpet.

His eyes flared with heat as he traced the curve of her breasts in the lacy white bra before he forced his gaze downward and began unsnapping her jeans. His head was bent, his black hair inches from her face, his eyelashes dark fans against his tanned skin as he slid the zipper downward.

"Nick," Charlene breathed.

He glanced up, his fingers going still on her waistband.

"You're wearing more clothes than I am."

He smiled slowly, closing the distance between them to slick his tongue over her bottom lip. "So take them off," he murmured.

She fumbled with the shirt buttons, breathing rapidly while her heartbeat pounded faster. She reached the button at his waistband and he let go of her jeans to grab his shirt and pull it free.

She reached behind her and unhooked her bra, shrugging her shoulders to let it fall free.

Nick reached for her, pulling her against him, skin-to-skin, and kissed her.

"I feel as if the world is still spinning," Charlene confided an hour later as they sat on her bed, a tray of food between them.

"Why is that?" Nick held out a bite of scone, dripping with butter and jam.

"Mmm." Charlene opened her mouth, chewed and swallowed. "These are heavenly. What did you say the name of the bakery is?"

"Mary Mac's. Hold still." Nick leaned over and licked the corner of her mouth. She tasted raspberry jam when he kissed her.

"Can we have these scones every Sunday?" she asked, caught by the intimacy of the moment.

"Absolutely." Nick grinned at her. "Marry me, babe, and I'll open an account there. You can have scones every day of the week if you want."

She laughed. "You don't have to bribe me. I already said I'd marry you—but the scones are definitely an added inducement," she added.

"Good to know what works," he said. "In case I need to bribe you in the future."

"You won't need bribes," she said softly. "Just ask."

His eyes heated. "You may regret that. I've built up a lot of hunger over the last few weeks."

Charlene's heart skipped, heat moving through her veins. "We've just spent hours in this bed. Aren't you exhausted?"

"Babe, I'm just catching my breath." He waggled his eyebrows at her suggestively and she laughed out loud. He grinned, clearly pleased he'd amused her. "I want to buy you something. What do you want for a wedding present? Diamonds? Rubies?"

"What?" Startled, Charlene searched his face and realized he was serious. "You don't have to buy me expensive things." She wanted to make it clear to Nick that his wealth wasn't why she loved him. But he clearly felt strongly about giving her a gift and she didn't want to disappoint him. She beamed, certain she had the perfect idea.

"There is something I'd love to have," she told him.

"You've got it," he said instantly. "What is it?"

"I would absolutely love it if we could set up a college fund for the triplets," she said earnestly.

He stared at her. "You want me to give the girls money for college?" he said slowly, eyeing her.

"Yes." She nodded emphatically. "Please," she added.

A slow smile curved his mouth. "You're something else, darlin'." He pressed a passionate kiss against her lips. "Any suggestions as to how big the fund should be?"

"No, you're the financial expert." She was still reeling from that kiss. "Oh, wait." She sat bolt upright, excited. "What if we ask the wedding guests to contribute to the girls' college fund in lieu of gifts for us?" She waved her hand at the comfortable, expensive furnishings in his big bedroom. "You have a whole houseful of stuff. What could we possibly need that you don't already have?"

He smiled, his expression tender. "There's nothing I need that I don't already have—now that I have you." He kissed her, wrapping his arms around her and rolling with her on the big bed until she was beneath him. "I think it's a great idea. Let's do it. We'll tell Lana and John this week."

"Good," she managed to say.

She felt surrounded by him—safe, loved, cherished and infinitely desired.

"I love you," she murmured, seeing the instant blaze of heat and fierce emotion in his eyes, just before he covered her mouth with his and the whole world fell away.

* * * * *

*Don't miss the next chapter in the
new Special Edition continuity*
**FORTUNES OF TEXAS:
RETURN TO RED ROCK**
*William Fortune, Jr. has just moved to Red Rock,
giving up his lucrative career in Los Angeles
to become a rancher. Part of the lure is
beautiful artist Isabella Mendoza.
But she believes he's just playing cowboy—
and playing her. Is he a true Texan?
Or just too good to be true?
Find out in*
A REAL LIVE COWBOY
by
Judy Duarte
*On sale April 2009,
wherever Silhouette Books are sold.*

*Celebrate 60 years of pure
reading pleasure with Harlequin®!
Silhouette® Romantic Suspense is celebrating
with the glamour-filled, adrenaline-charged series*
LOVE IN 60 SECONDS
*starting in April 2009.
Six stories that promise to bring the glitz of
Las Vegas, the danger of revenge, the mystery
of a missing diamond, family scandals and
ripped-from-the-headlines intrigue.
Get your heart racing as love happens
in sixty seconds!*

Enjoy a sneak peek of
USA TODAY *bestselling author
Marie Ferrarella's*
THE HEIRESS'S 2-WEEK AFFAIR
*Available April 2009
from Silhouette® Romantic Suspense.*

Eight years ago Matt Shaffer had vanished out of Natalie Rothchild's life, leaving behind a one-line note tucked under a pillow that had grown cold: *I'm sorry, but this just isn't going to work.*

That was it. No explanation, no real indication of remorse. The note had been as clinical and compassionless as an eviction notice, which, in effect, it had been, Natalie thought as she navigated through the morning traffic. Matt had written the note to evict her from his life.

She'd spent the next two weeks crying, breaking down without warning as she walked down the street, or as she sat staring at a meal she couldn't bring herself to eat.

Candace, she remembered with a bittersweet pang, had tried to get her to go clubbing in order to get her to forget about Matt.

She'd turned her twin down, but she did get her act together. If Matt didn't think enough of their relationship to try to contact her, to try to make her understand why he'd changed so radically from lover to stranger, then to hell with him. He was dead to her, she resolved. And he'd remained that way.

Until twenty minutes ago.

The adrenaline in her veins kept mounting.

Natalie focused on her driving. Vegas in the daylight wasn't nearly as alluring, as magical and glitzy as it was after dark. Like an aging woman best seen in soft lighting, Vegas's imperfections were all visible in the daylight. Natalie supposed that was why people like her sister didn't like to get up until noon. They lived for the night.

Except that Candace could no longer do that.

The thought brought a fresh, sharp ache with it.

"Damn it, Candy, what a waste," Natalie murmured under her breath.

She pulled up before the Janus casino. One of the three valets currently on duty came to life and made a beeline for her vehicle.

"Welcome to the Janus," the young attendant said cheerfully as he opened her door with a flourish.

"We'll see," she replied solemnly.

As he pulled away with her car, Natalie looked up at the casino's logo. Janus was the Roman god with two faces, one pointed toward the past, the other facing the future. It struck her as rather ironic, given what she was doing here, seeking out someone from her past in order to get answers so that the future could be settled.

The moment she entered the casino, the Vegas phenomena took hold. It was like stepping into a world where time did not matter or even make an appearance. There was only a sense of "now."

Because in Natalie's experience she'd discovered that bartenders knew the inner workings of any establishment they worked for better than anyone else, she made her way to the first bar she saw within the casino.

The bartender in attendance was a gregarious man in his early forties. He had a quick, sexy smile, which was probably one of the main reasons he'd been hired. His name tag identified him as Kevin.

Moving to her end of the bar, Kevin asked, "What'll it be, pretty lady?"

"Information." She saw a dubious look cross his brow. To counter that, she took out her badge. Granted she wasn't here in an official capacity, but Kevin didn't need to know that. "Were you on duty last night?"

Kevin began to wipe the gleaming black surface of the bar. "You mean during the gala?"

"Yes."

The smile gracing his lips was a satisfied one. Last night had obviously been profitable for him, she judged. "I caught an extra shift."

She took out Candace's photograph and carefully

placed it on the bar. "Did you happen to see this woman there?"

The bartender glanced at the picture. Mild interest turned to recognition. "You mean Candace Rothchild? Yeah, she was here, loud and brassy as always. But not for long," he added, looking rather disappointed. There was always a circus when Candace was around, Natalie thought. "She and the boss had at it and then he had our head of security escort her out."

She latched on to the first part of his statement. "They argued? About what?"

He shook his head. "Couldn't tell you. Too far away for anything but body language," he confessed.

"And the head of security?" she asked.

"He got her to leave."

She leaned in over the bar. "Tell me about him."

"Don't know much," the bartender admitted. "Just that his name's Matt Shaffer. Boss flew him in from L.A. where he was head of security for Montgomery Enterprises."

There was no avoiding it, she thought darkly. She was going to have to talk to Matt. The thought left her cold. "Do you know where I can find him right now?"

Kevin glanced at his watch. "He should be in his office. On the second floor, toward the rear." He gave her the numbers of the rooms where the monitors that kept watch over the casino guests as they tried their luck against the house were located.

Taking out a twenty, she placed it on the bar. "Thanks for your help."

Kevin slipped the bill into his vest pocket. "Any time, lovely lady," he called after her. "Any time."

She debated going up the stairs, then decided on the elevator. The car that took her up to the second floor was empty. Natalie stepped out of the elevator, looked around to get her bearings and then walked toward the rear of the floor.

"Into the Valley of Death rode the six hundred," she silently recited, digging deep for a line from a poem by Tennyson. Wrapping her hand around a brass handle, she opened one of the glass doors and walked in.

The woman whose desk was closest to the door looked up. "You can't come in here. This is a re-stricted area."

Natalie already had her ID in her hand and held it up. "I'm looking for Matt Shaffer," she told the woman.

God, even saying his name made her mouth go dry. She was supposed to be over him, to have moved on with her life. What happened?

The woman began to answer her. "He's—"

"Right here."

The deep voice came from behind her. Natalie felt every single nerve ending go on tactical alert at the same moment that all the hairs at the back of her neck stood up. Eight years had passed, but she would have recognized his voice anywhere.

* * * * *

*Why did Matt Shaffer leave
heiress-turned-cop Natalie Rothchild?
What does he know about the death
of Natalie's twin sister?
Come and meet these two reunited lovers
and learn the secrets of the Rothchild family in
THE HEIRESS'S 2-WEEK AFFAIR
by USA TODAY bestselling author
Marie Ferrarella.
The first book in Silhouette® Romantic Suspense's
wildly romantic new continuity,
LOVE IN 60 SECONDS!
Available April 2009.*

CELEBRATE
60 YEARS
OF PURE READING PLEASURE
WITH **HARLEQUIN**®!

**Look for Silhouette®
Romantic Suspense in April!**

Love In 60 Seconds

Bright lights. Big city. Hearts in overdrive.

Silhouette® Romantic Suspense is celebrating
Harlequin's 60th Anniversary with six stories that
promise to bring readers the glitz of Las Vegas,
the danger of revenge, the mystery of a missing
diamond, and family scandals.

**Look for the first title, *The Heiress's 2-Week Affair*
by *USA TODAY* bestselling author
Marie Ferrarella, on sale in April!**

His 7-Day Fiancée by **Gail Barrett**	May
The 9-Month Bodyguard by **Cindy Dees**	June
Prince Charming for 1 Night by **Nina Bruhns**	July
Her 24-Hour Protector by **Loreth Anne White**	August
5 minutes to Marriage by **Carla Cassidy**	September

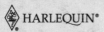

The Inside Romance newsletter has a NEW look for the new year!

Same great content, brand-new look!

The Inside Romance newsletter is a FREE quarterly newsletter highlighting our upcoming series releases and promotions!

Click on the Inside Romance link on the front page of **www.eHarlequin.com** or e-mail us at insideromance@harlequin.ca to sign up to receive your FREE newsletter today!

You can also subscribe by writing to us at: HARLEQUIN BOOKS Attention: Customer Service Department P.O. Box 9057, Buffalo, NY 14269-9057

Please allow 4-6 weeks for delivery of the first issue by mail.

REQUEST YOUR FREE BOOKS!

2 FREE NOVELS PLUS 2 FREE GIFTS!

SPECIAL EDITION®

Life, Love and Family!

YES! Please send me 2 FREE Silhouette Special Edition® novels and my 2 FREE gifts (gifts are worth about $10). After receiving them, if I don't wish to receive any more books, I can return the shipping statement marked "cancel." If I don't cancel, I will receive 6 brand-new novels every month and be billed just $4.24 per book in the U.S. or $4.99 per book in Canada, plus 25¢ shipping and handling per book and applicable taxes, if any*. That's a savings of at least 15% off the cover price! I understand that accepting the 2 free books and gifts places me under no obligation to buy anything. I can always return a shipment and cancel at any time. Even if I never buy another book from Silhouette, the two free books and gifts are mine to keep forever.

235 SDN EEYU   335 SDN EEY6

Name	(PLEASE PRINT)

Address	Apt. #

City	State/Prov.	Zip/Postal Code

Signature (if under 18, a parent or guardian must sign)

Mail to the Silhouette Reader Service:
IN U.S.A.: P.O. Box 1867, Buffalo, NY 14240-1867
IN CANADA: P.O. Box 609, Fort Erie, Ontario L2A 5X3

Not valid to current subscribers of Silhouette Special Edition books.

Want to try two free books from another line?
Call 1-800-873-8635 or visit www.morefreebooks.com.

* Terms and prices subject to change without notice. N.Y. residents add applicable sales tax. Canadian residents will be charged applicable provincial taxes and GST. Offer not valid in Quebec. This offer is limited to one order per household. All orders subject to approval. Credit or debit balances in a customer's account(s) may be offset by any other outstanding balance owed by or to the customer. Please allow 4 to 6 weeks for delivery. Offer available while quantities last.

Your Privacy: Silhouette is committed to protecting your privacy. Our Privacy Policy is available online at www.eHarlequin.com or upon request from the Reader Service. From time to time we make our lists of customers available to reputable third parties who may have a product or service of interest to you. If you would prefer we not share your name and address, please check here. ☐

SSE08R

You're invited to join our Tell Harlequin Reader Panel!

By joining our new reader panel you will:

- Receive Harlequin® books—they are FREE and yours to keep with no obligation to purchase anything!
- Participate in fun online surveys
- Exchange opinions and ideas with women just like you
- Have a say in our new book ideas and help us publish the best in women's fiction

In addition, you will have a chance to win great prizes and receive special gifts!
See Web site for details. Some conditions apply.
Space is limited.

To join, visit us at

www.TellHarlequin.com.

Silhouette®

COMING NEXT MONTH

Available March 31, 2009